...For All Eternity

TALES OF THE SEVEN DEADLY SINS

Edited by

A. W. Gifford &
Jennifer L. Gifford

Dark Opus Press
P.O. Box 1013
Grayson, Ga 30017

www.betenoiremagazine.com

...For All Eternity is published by Dark Opus Press a division of Charm Noir Omnimedia P.O Box 1013, Grayson, Ga 30017

ISBN-13: 978-0615727363
ISBN-10: 0615727360

Interior artwork provided by Chaz Kemp. For more of his work visit his website: www.chazkemp.com

Contents

Introduction – Jennifer L. Gifford   *1*

Envy
A Fragment of Shadow – Renee Carter Hall   7

Gluttony
Zion – Michael Beers   17

Greed
Hearts of Gold – Die Booth   29

Lust
Lecherous – Marten Hoyle   41

Pride
The Corpse Road – Christian Larsen   53

Sloth
Deadweight – Ken MacGregor   65

Wrath
Mauschwitz – Brandon French   71

Introduction

*"Sin begets sin...it engenders vice by repetition of the same acts...result-
ing in perverse inclinations, which cloud conscience and corrupt the concrete
judgment of good and evil...reproducing itself and reinforcing itself..."*

-exerpts from Catechism of the Catholic Church, 1865

A prideful stance. A lying tongue. Hands that spill innocent blood. A heart that plots evil. Bodies engaging in ungodly mischief. Being a witness of deceit. Sowing discord for folly and fun. *Superbia. Avaritia. Luxuria. Invidia. Gula. Ira. Acedia.* The Seven Deadly Sins. In the Book of Proverbs, King Solomon states that there are 'six things the Lord hateth, and the seventh His soul detesteth."

The cardinal vices that canonize humanity's fall into sin. Sin, humanities innate flaw that negates our sinful actions and ultimate consequences, is rooted in wickedness. From a biblical perspective, we are all sinners, divinely made and destined to commit unscrupulous behavior. One needs only to look at their thoughts and deeds over a single days period to confirm our own sins, yet we live in a state of detached aloofness — as if acknowledging the fact that we sin, yet being vague about the types of sins we commit, we are somehow less accountable for them. Even in the presence of our own personal evil, we still attempt to justify our wickedness with airs of altruism. As humans, we're all capable of unspeakable things, yet still struggle in vain to refrain from sin.

Popular as a theme in the Bible, captured by artists like De Morgan, and popular authors like C.S. Lewis, the Seven Deadly Sins are prevalent in religion, art, and literature, taking root in our culture and psyche.

The definition of each of the sins is both a spiritual and moral process that continues to evolve over time. Nearly two dozen sub-categories of emotional flaws were eventually narrowed down into a simple seven by Pope Gregory I in 590 A.D.

This narrowed down list of depravities is the scope that defines literature today.

Lust is the carnal intensity of desire. Desire for money, fame, power, and sex. Lust blinds us of true love. The sinful need of over indulgence and over consumption are hallmarks of Gluttony. It's wastefulness is a bi-product of our own selfishness and self servitude. Greed is the sin of excess, a sin of instantaneous rapture from the gratifications of material possessions. Greed is a gateway to violence, trickery, and manipulation. Obliviousness to what is morally just and laziness are traits of Sloth. Wrath is symbolic of uncontrolled rage and hatred, and the self destructiveness that emerges out of the chaotic anger gives birth to self righteousness. Wicked discontentment and jealousy encompass Envy, with its need to covet finding its origins all the way to the Bible's Ten Commandments. Pride is the longing to be more, to have more, to be more than those around us. It's the only sin whose moniker mimics Lucifer's own conceited battle with God — pride goeth before the fall — that gives the price for succumbing to smug arrogance, and that's the damnation of the soul.

The objectionable vices surrounding the Seven Deadly Sins challenge our culture and spirituality , and defines our moral compass. They corrupt and converge within our minds and hearts, and threaten our mortality and soul.

— Jennifer L. Gifford
October, 2012

A Fragment of Shadow

RENEE CARTER HALL

In the right hands, Giuliano thought, glass could sing. With the right breath and the right vision to shape it, it could be a clear, sweet voice of beauty in a rough, dissonant world.

Today, though, the glass was stubbornly silent, and Giuliano had sent his young assistant away, preferring to stir the molten glass himself as he brooded. The morning's completed pieces were in the annealing chamber, but he made no move to check them as they cooled. There were times—rare, blessèd hours—when he could feel the glass shaping itself to his will, every curve and flourish an extension of his thoughts. This morning had not been one of those times.

Giuliano heard soft footsteps behind him and knew without turning who had come. Paolo, of course, dependable as the sun chasing away a storm. Paolo was a lampworker, one who twisted and hammered the soft glass instead of blowing it. Beads were his specialty, and he often made rosaries, a work that suited his quiet temperament. While he was merely ten years Giuliano's junior, he held so much of the freshness of youth that visitors sometimes thought him an apprentice.

Paolo glanced around the studio. "Matteo off stealing sweetmeats again?"

"I sent him away."

"Ah." Paolo eyed him. "If you are occupied—"

"No." Giuliano wiped his face with a cloth. "No, it's all right."

"I've been working with the conciatore, trying new formulas for the colors. I wanted to show you."

It was easy to be friends with Paolo. His ambitions were humble, his talent masterful without rising to the level of genius. He was no threat to anyone's dream.

Paolo showed him a handful of beads the color of the spring sky. Giuliano took one and held it up to the afternoon light slanting in from the window. "Marvelous. Are they all so pure?"

"As best I could make them. I could have him make a batch of it for you, if you like."

Giuliano's mouth twisted into a wry smile. "To what end? Nothing I birth these days deserves to live."

Paolo nodded. "What news, then, of Silvio?"

Giuliano turned back to the glass, feeling the furnace's heat wash over him.

Silvio.

The best glassmaker in Murano, or so word always went. Oh, he knew one man's thought of what was best could differ from another's as widely as the moon from the sun. But every word of praise was still another drop of poison.

Giuliano sighed. "Commissioned by the doge. All the glassware for his grand table, and gifts for the finest families of Venice."

"Mm." Paolo bent his dark head a moment. "Sounds like far too much work for my taste."

Trust Paolo to make a jest out of it. Still, he found himself smiling.

"There, now." Paolo returned the smile. "A foul mood spoils the work, you know."

"And how do you keep yours so fair, my friend?"

Paolo looked at the stone floor. "I think of the purpose for which I fashion the glass. I imagine the prayers that will be said, and the comfort my work might give. It is no longer merely glass then, and the work—well, the work is prayer itself. Praise, and thanks, and joy." He paused, and though his voice was still light, he spoke more quietly. "Is it not so with you?"

Giuliano said nothing. After a moment, Paolo nodded. "Adriana asked me to invite you for dinner next week. Her sister Francesca is planning a visit." He paused. "That is to say, her unmarried sister, the one who is quite fond of the arts?"

"I expect I'll be busy here."

"Of course. How could any woman compare with the great joy you take from your work?" Paolo smiled, but there was something of sadness in his eyes. "I'll see you later."

Giuliano waited until Paolo's footsteps faded, and then took out the last goblet he'd blown that morning. Now that he was holding it, he could feel that it was even thicker than he'd remembered, and as he looked at it more closely, he saw the tiny air bubble just below where the rim widened more than it should.

He opened his hand and let the goblet fall.

Stomach sour and head aching, he turned back to the hot glass and began again. Let them all have Silvio, if that was what they wanted. Most of them only knew titles and lineages anyway. Who among Silvio's fanciers truly knew art? Fat nobles with full purses and empty heads, every one.

A hissing began in the back of his head, a sensation that was neither sound nor pain. He shook his head a bit, mopped sweat from his face, and kept on, completing one piece, setting it aside to cool, and starting another.

He'd been to the parties, standing at the fringes while noblemen and women alike fawned over the maestro like eager hounds. He'd seen the crowds at the shops on the days Silvio's latest work arrived, while his own pieces gathered dust on the shelves.

And yet that was not the worst. Were Silvio a talentless fraud, it would be simple to wave his fame away. But the maestro's work was like air given shape: delicate, crystalline fantasies that made one want to laugh like a child at their wonder, to weep like a woman at their beauty.

His breaths came harder now, as if an iron band encircled him, but he poured everything into the glass, everything of himself, everything he could give.

Then, all at once, the hissing grew to a roar, as if waves crashed inside his skull. The pipe fell from his grasp, and the forgotten glass cooled and cracked as he dropped to his knees and clapped his hands to his temples.

...free...

...free...

...free...free...free...

The roaring became a chorus of overlapping whispers, the sounds sliding over each other like twining snakes. It was said that great geniuses sometimes went mad, but Giuliano suddenly felt an overwhelming desire to be mediocre.

He felt something in his mind like water bubbling over stones. Like laughter.

...master...

...great master...

...wants to be great...

...wants to be first...

...wants to be only...

Giuliano shook his head, as if the whispers were water he could pound from his ears. The voices only grew stronger.

...so it shall be...

He could almost feel the sounds on his skin, feather-light and blade-sharp. Giuliano shivered. Was he hearing angels? Demons? Or the Devil himself?

Then his gaze fell on the cooled glass at the end of his pipe. The goblet was cracked and warped, flattened on one side where he'd dropped it.

And it was black.

He reached for the piece, breaking it off without bothering to heat it again. The jagged edge looked like a row of dark teeth.

Black glass. He staggered to his feet and held the piece to the light, expecting a smoky translucence or a greenish tint. But the glass seemed to pull the light into itself, swallowing it in darkness, like a shadow made solid.

Shaking, he peered into the annealing chamber. They were all black.

His mouth went dry, and for a moment he forgot the strange chorus in his mind. No one had ever made such things as these.

Not even Silvio.

✝

"Remarkable," Paolo breathed. "I think of how wonderful it would look with gold, but the more I look at it, the more it seems to need no decoration. The form, Giuliano—how did you get it so fine? It moves like water." Carefully he picked up a vase, turning it in his hands. "You must have just finished. It's still warm."

Curious, Giuliano brushed his fingertips over the base of a goblet. Though it should have long since cooled, the glass felt warm against his skin.

As if it were alive.

He shook off the thought. There was nothing here but some fluke of composition that would give him, at last, the name he'd sought for so long. Those voices were merely frustration and overwork, a brain-fever broken and passed.

Paolo placed the vase back on the shelf. "I suppose they're all going to the shops, then?"

"Almost all of them." Giuliano smiled. "After you have your choice."

A moment passed before Paolo could speak. "I couldn't—"

"You can. Think of it as payment for putting up with a bitter old fool."

"Come now, you're not so old." Paolo grinned. "All right, then." He surveyed the row of glassware, settling finally on a small wine glass.

"You *would* take the simplest one."

"Because anything finer would make the rest of my home look like a peasant's cottage by comparison." He ran his fingertips lightly over the glass. "Besides, even in such a simple form, it seems to... sing, somehow. A very old, alluring song." He gazed at it, then blinked and looked up as if jarred from a trance. "I must get back to my own humble work, I suppose. Thank you, Giuliano. It's a rare gift."

Once he was gone, Giuliano studied the remaining pieces. He should make sure the glass could be duplicated before allowing any of it out into the public. And yet...

Giuliano reached for an elaborate goblet, by far the finest he'd ever made. He allowed himself one last moment to admire its perfection, then called Matteo over from sweeping.

The boy's eyes widened at the sight of the glass, but he gulped and looked back down at the stones. "Sí, maestro?"

Giuliano smiled and passed him the goblet. "Have this sent over to Maestro Silvio. A gift for him, the first of my new design, with my compliments on his own fine work."

✝

If the first day had been heaven, the next two were hell. Though he made countless attempts, he could not replicate the glass, and the conciatore claimed nothing in that particular batch had been unusual.

Paolo brought a basket to him at midday with wine, fresh bread, and figs. "Matteo says you haven't slept."

"Matteo sleeps enough for both of us." Giuliano stirred the molten glass. He'd ordered the conciatore to leave the manganese out of this batch, in hopes that some impurity had created the color.

Paolo sighed. "I know it must be difficult—"

"Difficult? It's impossible. That color can put my work in every noble's home, but if I can't make it again..." He paused. "Has Silvio said anything of the piece I sent him? Has he shown it to anyone else? I've had no word from him. I suppose at last he has nothing to say, eh?"

Paolo's face went ashen. "I suppose so. He died last night."

There had been no mark on Silvio, no hint of sickness, no trace of poison in the wine he drank. All around the island, noblemen and shopkeepers alike muttered about *malocchio* and made signs against the evil eye. Some wondered if Silvio had been too good, if he had offended God with the perfection of his work and the admiration of so many.

Giuliano cared nothing for such gossip. He had work to do. Day after day, he sweated at his furnace, eager to take Silvio's place in the shops, but still the color eluded him. Every time, the glass was ordinary, and every time, in the back of his mind, he heard laughter, though whether it was the voice of the glass or his own submerged self mocking him, he could not tell. When Matteo interrupted him with some foolish question, he snatched up a spoiled vase and threw it at the boy. The vase smashed on the floor, and Matteo skittered away like a rabbit.

Giuliano rubbed his eyes and went back to the shelf of black glass. He'd been able to retrieve the goblet sent to Silvio, and now he admired it bitterly, wondering if it truly was to be his best work. The collectors who should have been buying it and dozens of others like it were busy outbidding each other for Silvio's final pieces.

He picked up the goblet, savoring its delicate weight in his hand. As before, the glass was oddly warm.

Then it pulsed under his fingers.

He threw the goblet to the ground, a strangled cry rising in his throat. The glass broke into three large pieces, and as he watched, the pieces shivered, like the throb of a heartbeat.

He stared at them for several moments, mind churning. They did not move again. Perhaps he had imagined it. He had felt nothing like that with Paolo's glass...

Paolo.

But certainly it had been mere coincidence, the gift to Silvio and the maestro's death—

A low chuckle seeped into his mind, and the glass pulsed again.

He turned and ran into the streets.

Paolo was not at his furnace; his apprentice said he had gone home. Giuliano rushed down the next street, red-faced and frantic, ignoring the stares of those he passed. Let people think him mad. Perhaps he was.

He burst past the cringing maid at the door. "Paolo?"

They were at the table. Paolo lay on the floor, eyes open and staring, his wife weeping over him. Beyond Paolo's outstretched fingertips, the black goblet lay in a spreading pool of dark red wine.

✝

Two nights later, Giuliano sat at his bench, the only light coming from the furnace as the fire died to glowing coals. Paolo's wife had given him one of the rosaries, among the last works his friend had fashioned, and he ran the beads aimlessly through his fingers.

Had he summoned a demon? Or was it merely himself, his own darkness given shape? Could such a thing even be cast out, then, if it were part of him?

His hands shook, and the glass beads clattered. He held them close to the firelight. Pure, beautiful color, as simple and sincere as its maker. Paolo had put the best of himself into his work, and he... He had poured evil into his.

Giuliano squinted at one bead. There was a tiny bubble near its edge. If it had been his own work, he would have hated it for such a flaw. Had Paolo loved it in spite of that? Or even because of it? A bit of his friend's breath, perhaps, trapped forever in glass.

Trapped...

Giuliano got to his feet and stoked the fire. Paolo's wine glass, the vase, the fragments of Silvio's goblet—each piece from the shelf melted into the flames. When the glass was stirred and ready, he gathered it onto the warmed pipe, closed his eyes, prayed, and exhaled.

He allowed himself the anger, allowed himself the frustration, the bitterness, the hatred of all who possessed what he dreamed of. He felt the familiar darkness rise in him and did not push it away. Instead, he let it flow through him, and when the roaring began in his head again, he gathered it into a single breath and sent it out into the glass.

Paolo, forgive me. You admired the work of a demon in a man's shape.

At last, spent and shaking, he dared to look at the sphere of cooling glass. It was dark, as the other glass had been, but within it a greater blackness swirled like smoke. He watched it closely over the hours as it cooled, but no cracks appeared.

The voices were silent. The voices were gone. Clutching Paolo's rosary, he stumbled to the straw mattress in the corner and slept.

✝

"Papà!" Gemma ran to her father, and Guiliano scooped her up in his arms and lifted her into the air until she squealed with laughter.

"Careful, love, she's just eaten." But Francesca was smiling as she joined them.

"We came to see you make glass, Papà."

"Then you shall see it." Guiliano held her just a moment longer before putting her down. "But you must stay close so you don't get hurt, all right?"

The child nodded, her brown eyes wide and solemn, but Giuliano knew well enough that in moments she'd be off poking into whatever she shouldn't. Gemma was curious as a young goat, and she had about as much respect for rules.

Giuliano turned to Francesca. "The doctor said it was all right to come?"

"I didn't ask." She smiled and put up a slim hand to stop his protest. "I'm fine. But your child is restless," she added, laying a hand on her gown, "and I wanted fresh air."

"Not a lazy one, then. He must take after his father." Giuliano glanced back at Gemma. She'd found a crate of straw and was throwing handfuls of it into the air. He chuckled and shook his head. More sweeping for Matteo — if his apprentice ever came back from flirting with the shopkeepers' daughters.

Francesca crossed to the shelf that held the completed pieces. "These are the newest, then? They're lovely. They could be crystal." She rested a hand on his arm, and he drew her close. "The work of a master," she whispered.

Giuliano laid his palm at the rise of her gown, where he could feel the child move within her. "There are things in the world more marvelous than what even a maestro can make."

He heard Gemma laugh. He turned, expecting to see her peeking out at them from behind a stack of crates. Instead, a wooden box lay open at her feet, its lock rusted by the salty air. And in her hands she held a bubble of glass, watching dark fog dance within it.

"Gemma." His first try was barely a whisper, and she did not hear. He swallowed, heart racing. "Gemma!"

The shout startled her, and the sphere slipped from her hands. It seemed to hang in the air for the space of a breath, and in that moment, he thought he heard echoes of low, hungry laughter.

…free…

The glass shattered on the stones.

✝

Renee Carter Hall *works as a medical transcriptionist by day and as a writer, poet, and artist all the time. Her short fiction has appeared in a variety of publications, including* Strange Horizons, Black Static, *the anthology* Bewere the Night, *and the* Anthro Dreams *podcast. She lives in West Virginia with her husband, their cat, and a ridiculous number of creative works-in-progress. Readers can find more about her and her work at* www.reneecarterhall.com.

Zion

MICHAEL BEERS

People swarmed to Promised Mount, hoping to find someone to lead them out of this world of chaos. The sun was high as the stage was set for a speech from their beloved prophet.

And, as he approached the stage to plenty of cheers, Propet raised his hand and began, "My fellow Consumers, Consumus, our lovely homeworld, is dead. We must move on to Zion!"

Propet pointed towards the large yellow ships with checkerboard stripes behind him. They were there should anyone in the crowd follow Propet to the promised land. The engines let off a low hum which Propet did not let interrupt his speech, yet it was a reminder they were still there.

Many of the people in the crowd had grown on the legends of Zion, a paradise full of nature. A land of lush color and vibrant fruit. From sea to shining sea, Zion was meant to be a utopia for all to live in.

It was the planet of their ancestors, who came on large yellow ships to this world in hopes of expanding their ways of life.

However, the planet Consumus was a dry and barren land full of grey. The skies were clouded with the smoke of assembly plants. The ground was barren of color, bearing no fruit for people to feed upon. The plants, if there were any that survived, were all sickly and wilted.

And the people were starving for a better life.

They had come in hopes Propet had an answer for their horrific world.

And, as his first statement proved to the people, it was an appealing answer indeed.

Zion was the promised land of Consumus, the paradise of fruitfulness. They had been fed on this story throughout their lives and, as Propet proved, knew it was the only option available.

It's the only place people like me can begin a new life.

If only I wasn't too late to save my son.

The thoughts of Propet's son clouded his mind, unable to notice the crowd was cheering for him to continue. Eventually, their loud cries broke through his mind and Propet was able to shake off the ghosts of his past. He knew it would be easy to convince them if their cries were able to pull him away from *that*.

Propet continued, "Consumus—our lovely home planet—is held ransom by the vile ways of the Earthmen. Only the Corporati, the heads of all business, remain above us by ripping our jobs away from us and leaving us no way to earn a living. They have moved their corporations to different planets in hopes of lower costs and higher profits. But, they have only robbed us of the fracti we use to feed ourselves with rising prices! They have forced us to take out loans on our lives within the Earthen institutions called banks. And yet, when we rely on these banks to provide for us, they only rob us of more fracti.

"They say we are able to live a normal life."

"But, how can we spend if we cannot earn?"

"How can we grow if we cannot feed on the fruit of our labors?"

The crowd cried out again in enthusiasm to Propet's argument, knowing he was strong enough to say what others could not. Though there were some not swayed by Propet's words, Propet knew they would come around eventualy. By the end of his speech, everyone would be dying to move on to Zion.

Everyone always did.

Propet allowed the cries of the crowd long enough before resuming, "The Corporati took away our wealth because of this new style of 'economy' from the Terrans. They expect us to borrow money we cannot pay back in order to live. The fracti has become the fruit we feed upon."

Propet stretched his arms out to encompass the entire crowd. "AND IF WE CAN'T PAY, THEN THEY TAKE EVERYTHING BUT OUR LIVES!"

Propet looked to the left side of the crowd. "Our homes!"

Propet looked to the right side of the crowd, he continued. "Our vehicles!"

Propet looked to the center of the crowd, he exclaimed. "Our food!"

Propet slammed his fist on the podium, crying out with his eyes, "Nothing of ours is exempt from their greed!"

Including my son...

Propet had to stop for a moment because thoughts of his son interrupted his speech.

My God, what would he think of me now?

But, he wasn't strong enough for this world. Perhaps he would understand...

Regaining his composure, Propet wiped a small tear away from his eye. He continued to the crowds, "The banks, the business leaders, have grown so powerful they own our lives—body and soul!"

Pointing out at the crowd, Propet dramatically drew his audience deeper into his dialogue. "Many of you older Consumers remember when work was ample, vehicles were reliable, homes were warm, and food was plenty. Now, we are forced into unemployment, immobility, homelessness, and," Propet paused, remembering the ribs showing on his son's body, before he gasped out, "starvation."

"The leaders of Consumus have left us barren without money to pay for our lives because we have become fruitless investments."

Sighing, Propet let out with a slight whisper, "Many of you have suffered because of this new slavery. I, too, am a victim of their shackles. Their crimes cannot be concealed from our eyes any longer." With tears in his eyes, Propet cried out, "Now, look at what their greed gives us!"

Propet removed his bright white robes, revealing a slender naked body to the masses. Though many were appalled he would reveal his nude body to the crowd, they could not ignore the effects starvation planted within his body. Sores and wounds covered his delicate flesh while scars marked where the world had feasted on him before. His frail, starved body was like a fruit past its ripeness.

Propet himself was even amazed at how bad his body looked. *There are so many scars on my body. And I look so weak.*

Just like he looked before he died.

"Fruitlessness has caused this to..."

Propet muttered as he choked back the tears, remembering what starvation had feasted upon. He thought of the little boy whom the doctors placed in his arms after he was born. It was the happiest day of Propet's life.

But, the image was corrupted. He could only think of holding the frail, starved body of his son in his arms as he died. It was the saddest day in Propet's life.

And my body is looking just like his before he died...

He looked out into the crowd and watched the little children play-ing in the fields as their parents watched on mesmerized by his words and the promise they held within them. He felt this feeling once be-fore, and seeing it tantalizing his soul yet again caused him to choke up in misery.

What am I doing here? I can't do this to them.

But, asking them to stay here would do the same thing.

Propet tried to cry out to the crowd, but the tears muffled the sound. "Think of what it will bring for you!" He covered his face, ashamed to show weakness to the crowd who now looked to them as their savior.

Someday, I will not be haunted by the image of my son.

But today is not that day.

Propet returned the bright white robe to his shoulders, ready to re-sume his speech once he regained his composure. "Our reliance upon the Coproati and the fracti force us to pay tolls to them to live. They feed themselves on our well-being. Our souls are like a delicious fruit to them, hoping it will fill their gluttonous stomachs.

"Ever since the Earthmen landed and taught the Corporati their life-style, our world has become a place where only the strong survive and the weak end up a victim of the system. We have become no better than the animals of the wilderness. But, who are they to determine who are the strong and who are the weak?"

Propet stopped for a moment, allowing the crowd's responses to fill the air.

"Yeah!"

"You said it!"

"Down with the Corporati!"

"To Utopia!"

"To paradise!"

"To Zion!"

That's it. I've got them now.

"I have witnessed firsthand—like many of you have—the destruct-ive force of their greed. And they toss us aside without a care, like the core of an apple!

"And," Propet stated, "My family—like many of yours—has expired thanks to their efforts.

Propet looked down at a family and pointed directly at them, first focusing on the tall, aged male, "They have done this to my father..."

He moved his hand to the tall, aged female, "They have done this to my mother..."

He moved his hand to the one holding a baby, "They have done this to my wife..."

He then moved his hand to the baby in the mother's arms. Propet stuttered the words out of his mouth, the memories of his son choking him. "They have...done this...to my..."

Propet tried to continue on, but the water welling up within his eyes prevented him from uttering the last word. It took every ounce of effort to move on before his sorrow drowned out his speech...

"They have done this to my son."

Propet turned from the crowd as he allowed their responses to fill the air. He no longer cared what they said. He had them convinced. The rest of this speech was all for show.

Yet, the words loomed over Propet's soul. Once the words left his lips, all he could envision were the faces of his family fading away. Propet felt powerless against the new Consumer machine which threatened his way of life, causing the expiration of his family: past, present, and future.

After all, Propet thought, *starvation feeds upon everyone, regardless of who they are. Those left behind would do anything to survive.*

I wish I wasn't strong enough to survive.

But, I'm still strong enough to do this.

God, what have I become?

Propet returned to his senses and could tell the crowd was completely swayed as his words whisked through the air. All of them were crying out in support of fleeing to Zion.

Propet gathered himself together and turned back to the podium, concluding his argument, "Many of our daughters and..." Though he could feel the ghostly visions of his son begin to haunt him, Propet forced himself on through the tears, "Our sons have died in a quest of gluttony. The pride of those who oppress us cannot stifle us any longer. We must leave now to prove once and for all our bodies can no longer be harvested for their gains. We must show them our souls are not for them to feast upon. And, my fellow Consumers, we must not stand idly while they continue to kill us. To utopia! To paradise! To Zion!"

The crowd cheered in mass agreement.

"To utopia! To paradise! To Zion!"

"To utopia. To paradise. To Zion," Propet echoed. He was now in control of the crowd. The audience was behind him and it was time for him to reap the results of his efforts. Though he had made the same promise to his son a long time ago, he pushed through the feelings that wanted to overwhelm him. It was time to reap the results of his efforts.

"My brothers and sisters..."

"To utopia!"

"...we must now allow the leaders of Consumus's businesses..."

"To paradise!"

"...to be the upper crust of society's pie..."

"To Zion!"

"...while the fruit of our world..."

"To utopia!"

"...is forced to starve."

"To paradise!"

"We must go to Zion..."

"To Zion!"

"...and create a utopia..."

"To utopia!"

"...a natural paradise..."

"To paradise!"

"...for all of us to thrive!"

"To Zion!"

"To utopia!"

"To utopia!"

"To paradise!"

"To paradise!"

"To Zion!"

"To Zion!"

The crowd began to march along behind Propet's guiding steps, herding themselves into the big yellow ships destined to take them to the planet Zion. Once the bellies of the ships were full, the ships headed towards their fruitful paradise.

However, Propet knew his job was far from done. They were there in the ships, but he needed to keep them focused on the ideal. There could be no turning back.

Propet stood before the masses on the ships and called out, "My dear Consumers, it seems in the excitement of the moment I forgot to see if you had any questions!" The crowd chuckled at Propet's error, since many of them knew what Zion looked like from the ancient tales. "If there is anything you want to know, please raise your hand and I will answer your questions."

As a multitude of hands arose, Propet pointed to a boy towards the front of the crowd who begged, "What does Zion look like?"

Propet laughed for a moment, then answered, "Well, little boy, Zion is the world of our dreams. The land promised to us by God himself. Its landscape is covered with food for all of us. The trees are fruitful and plenty, giving us fruit to feast upon. The rivers are clear and pure, full of fish to catch. The sun sets in the west and rises in the east, giving off a rainbow hue on the fruited plains, brightening the purple mountains, and making the amber waves of grain glow every morning and evening. Any good Consumer would agree Zion is truly our paradise."

Propet sighed and touched the boy's shoulder in hopes to conclude his answer. Yet, as he looked at him, he could see the young face he once knew. The boy was now on his father's shoulders, something Propet's own son loved. He felt his sorrow return as the male youngling looked down at him, realizing nothing in the world, not even this, would bring his son back.

Propet held back crying long enough for him to give off one last statement.

"I just wish my...I mean, I wish our families could see the promised land for themselves."

Propet looked up to the boy again, seeing the same bright eyes he watched become extinguished in his arms many years ago. The light of the ship shone from behind the boy now, giving him an otherworldly glow.

Propet could no longer hide the sorrow within himself.

All the vivid memories of his son flowed through his mind without yield: his first day, his first smile, his first steps, his first words, his first day at school, his first tears. His first time begging for food. His first ribs showing. His first sign of sunken eyes. His first sign of sores...

His last breath.

The boy beneath him looked so much like his son now. The same bright eyes. The same shaggy hair. The same strong cheekbones. The same frail body.

He was looking at his dead son.

No, it can't be...he's gone...I know he's gone...he died in my arms...why does his image haunt me?

Propet ran to a compartment towards the front of the big yellow ship, trying to escape the ghosts of his past. The youngling looked so much like his son, it scared him.

My God, what have I become?

With Propet gone, the crowd cheered on with the promise of their paradise, Zion, to lead them. A land where Consumers wouldn't have a care in the world. The land and God would provide for them.

Propet could hear the people singing of Zion for the rest of the trip. He couldn't even tell when the engines died down, signaling their arrival at Zion. Turning to the room's projector, he watched as the crowd became mesmerized by the shimmering surface and the lights of the landscape. Propet continued to stare at the screen, watching their reactions at seeing Zion through the windows for the first time in their lives. At first, they admired the new world.

Then, they noticed the street lights like neon trees.

They noticed the paved roads like oily paths.

They noticed the silver cars like metalic animals.

They noticed the skyscrapers like piercing mountains.

There was something rotten about the appearance of Zion.

Their paradise was infected with urbanization.

The crowd looked for their prophet to explain this perverse land-scape to them, but Propet was nowhere to be found...by them at least. The only words they could find to nourish their desires were harsh and electric.

"Welcome to Zion!"

"Please deposit one silver fractal or one Earth cent to enter the land of plenty!"

"Welcome to Zion!"

"Please deposit one silver fractal or one Earth cent..."

The crowd now realized they were merely sacrifices to appease the Corporati, their new gods. They wanted to pay the toll and try to be born again on Zion, but no one had a penny to pay to their now urb-anized utopia.

Propet turned and walked over to the captain to collect the bounty of his harvest.

Propet did not want to care about them anymore.

His job was done.

Yet the image of the youngling who asked him the question re-minded him of his own son. And what they did to him.

The captain entered from the cockpit, smiling at Propet. He then reached into his pocket and tossed a bag onto the metal table. The sound of the silver fracti within the bag echoed in the hollow room.

Hollow, just like myself. I'm merely their puppet to keep the people happy.

The captain broke through Propet's thoughts, complimenting, "You did well, salesman. A bigger haul than usual. They will make great slaves to build more cities on Zion."

"Thank you," was all Propet could mutter. A part of him was glad to be getting paid, but part of him wanted to fight back. He closed his eyes and thought about the boy whom asked him about Zion.

His son once asked him about Zion.

He told him it was a place where nature's beauty was unsurpassed.

Now, Propet helped to make it a place of manufactured ugliness.

I can't stand for this anymore. I need to end this now. In the name of my son, I need to end this now.

The captain crossed his arms and scowled at Propet. "Now, since your job is done, take your thirty silver fracti and get out." The sight of the captain like that frightened Propet. He knew the captain had orders to kill Propet if he would dare to rebel against him. He knew the captain would relish in such a treat. It had been a long time since the captain feasted upon killing others at the dining table of war.

"Sir," Propet stuttered out in a shaky voice, remembering the threat of death hanging over his head. "I...was...wondering...about the... sales...technique..."

"Ah, yes," the captain smiled, realizing where Propet was going to go with this line of questioning. There were several times Propet tried to step up and stop them. But, every time, the captain or someone like him was there to stop his deviant nature. He knew just the way to stop him, too. "The new advertisement campaign Marketing has come up with may end up cutting into your job, Propet. We were hoping to integrate you into it, if you are willing to continue getting paid, that is. After all, you're our big seller. We need you to help push the sales of migrants to Zion."

"Yeah...what if...what if we..."

"Propet," the captain stated while staring directly into Propet's eyes. He needed to end this line of questioning now before it went too far. But, he always did. "If you have any suggestions on how to improve our marketing technique, I suggest you either put it in writing and submit it to the Public Relations division or request a transfer there. Now," the captain moved closer to the sack of silver fracti. Picking it up, he swung the bag before him, tantalizing Propet with the money to forget his concerns. "Please take the money you rightfully earned. I'm betting you'll be able to buy some great food with it. Perhaps some steak...or even some shrimp...*or* something even better. But, please take it."

Propet snatched the silver out of the captain's hands and began to caress it lovingly, knowing it was the key to survival. He had enough money he could quit. He could go to Zion and buy a place to live. But, then, he could not afford food or drink. All he could do with his money anymore was adore how much he had.

"My...

"Please, salesman, don't do that here," interrupted the captain. "You creep me out when you do that. Just go do that in your room. It's only silver fracti after all."

Propet stopped, yet continued in his mind to recount the value it meant to him.

My God, how I adore thee...

The captain looked out and surveyed the steel and stone landscape of Zion, commenting, "I must say, Zion looks so much better without all that nature. After all, who ever saw any value in a piece of fruit?"

Propet just turned, leaving the captain to his solitude. He finally found a moment the memories of the past could not haunt him. When Propet held a sack of silver, he knew it should silence his stomach for a few more seconds of his sold-out existence.

✝

Michael Beers *is currently a graduate student at the University of Toledo where he is studying for his MA in Literature, where he hopes to concentrate in science fiction and fantasy literature. In his spare time, he writes science fiction and fantasy and enjoys travelling deep into the worlds of his mind.*

Hearts of Gold

DIE BOOTH

They say she can cure a toothache, or help you sleep, or find that which is lost. They say she can cause a drought to break, or grant you luck, or keep your sweetheart faithful. She can mend broken bones so the limb heals straight as a pike, and predict if your child will be a girl or a boy. She knows when you will die. They say she can fly.

✝

People said a lot of things about Mother Pellar and Walter de Aurum had heard most of them: the rumours that she owned a cloak of spider silk which rendered her invisible and that the laths in her cottage walls were of gold instead of wood. Looking around her parlour, he had his doubts. It was certain that she was skilled — there was much testament to her prowess at cures, charms and fortune telling — but he suspected that credulous folk greatly overestimated any power she held over them.

"And what brings you here today. *Sir.*"

She certainly looked her part, too. Although the little dwelling was swept and orderly enough it was shabby and that evidence of meagre means extended to the old maid's appearance. Dressed all in black, Mother Pellar wore not only a cap but also a hooded and veiled cape which revealed only her eyes, black as pips in a shrivelled apple, amidst her crepe of wrinkles.

"I come here in confidence." De Aurum paused and licked his lips. "I trust that you will keep that confidence."

The woman nodded, but the veil obscured enough of her expression that it was not a wholly comforting gesture. He continued slowly,

"There is a man of my district who has slighted me unforgivably. I wish for...recompense."

Checking her eyes for any signs of disapproval, de Aurum faced only the same black, unreadable mirrors. "I wish to bring about his ruin." He added, in case his subtlety had been lost on her.

"I can aid you."

"You must understand, the blackguard brought—" He fell to quiet with a frown as the old woman held up one hand in a silencing gesture.

"Your motivation is none of my concern, so long as you pay me my fee. I mean to say," the corners of her eyes crinkled further, as if under the veil she was smiling, "what just cause motivates you is none of my *business. Sir.*"

"Quite so."

There was something about her tone that de Aurum much objected to, but he needed her assistance, so it was best to be prudent the while. "And that fee would be?"

"Six gold crowns."

De Aurum couldn't have held his bark of laughter in if he'd tried. "Six gold crowns, for a piece of petty conjuring?"

"Six gold crowns for the ruin of your enemy, and there'll be no other cunning folk willing to help you with the like of that."

"For that payment, I highly doubt that."

The old woman leaned closer to de Aurum than he liked and he caught a whiff even over the smell of the fire of something herbal which would have been curiously pleasant if not for the circumstances.

"Those who do evil risk evil returning upon them. Only an experienced one would chance it. Or a fool."

De Aurum cleared his throat. "As I believe I made clear, this man deserves retribution. I am requesting no aid to evil."

"Yes, yes," Mother Pellar waved a hand once more and de Aurum felt the blood rise to his face. But she had already turned her back on him, shuffling over to her table and consulting a large grimoire laid out there which she made every appearance of being able to read. Noticing him peering over her shoulder, she did not attempt to disguise her obscuring hand and the only thing de Aurum was able to glance before she covered the text was a diagram of signs set inside a circle that meant nothing to him. She said, "So you want this charm?"

"I do."

"And you agree to my terms?"

De Aurum clenched his teeth so that they twisted a nutcracker squeak through his jaw. "I do."

"Then we have an accord."

✝

Impatience dictated he stay whilst Mother Pellar prepared his charm, but the old woman insisted that ingredients needed to be gathered and rituals performed and in the event it was a full week before de Aurum returned for his merchandise. Mother Pellar was waiting for him at her gate, as if she sensed his arrival or perhaps had been in wait for a while. Beckoning him inside the cottage, she presented de Aurum with a sealed bottle.

"This is to be hidden upon your rival's property."

"His house?" He took the bottle and regarded it dubiously. It made no sound when he shook it but when he held it up against the light of the fire, the contents showed dimly; viscous black against the green of the glass. Mother Pellar said,

"His house, or his grounds will do. Do not open it."

"What is inside?"

"That's nothing to concern you."

De Aurum pursed his lips. He tried another tactic.

"So, herbs and words have the power to influence men?"

Mother Pellar sat down in her chair next to the fire, without offering her guest a seat. She nodded.

"If you know the right ones."

"The right herbs, or words, or men?"

That got him a chuckle from beneath the black veil. It didn't do anything to lessen his conviction that Mother Pellar took advantage of gullible folk. And gullible was something that Walter de Aurum certainly was not. "And supposing your methods are so effective. Why does everybody not follow them?"

"Oh, because men mistrust change," The bows of her chair creaked and cracked against the floor as Mother Pellar rocked gently. "There's many a thing I know and put to use in my work as would benefit so-called learned men, if they ever had the time and inclination to listen to an old woman."

"Such as?"

The bottle had grown warm in his hand and now it seemed that whatever was inside it was retaining that warmth, multiplying it and radiating back into his skin. He set the bottle down on the table at his side, then changed his mind and picked it up again. Mother Pellar leaned her head to one side and said, "On account that something appears clean and smells fresh, does not equal that it is not tainted."

"And that is the extent of your wisdom?"

"The bite of a rat or fly can spread poison just as sure as the bite of a serpent, as can foul water. But an attercop won't harm nobody."

De Aurum smiled without mirth. "I suppose next you would have me dispense with consulting a physician for my ailments and come to you instead."

"Perhaps." The old woman ceased rocking in her chair and the sudden quiet was filled only with the crackling of the fire. "There was the matter, also, of payment."

De Aurum looked again at the little charm bottle in his hand, the stopper wrapped in black thread and sealed with wax. He said,

"Surely one as wise and good as you would have me think you would not put a price on such an instrument of justice as this?"

"And surely an honest gentleman of such means as yourself would not begrudge a person their living wage?" Mother Pellar leaned forward in her chair, bracing her knotted hands against her knees as she stood. From the shadow of the doorway a tabby cat slid, flattening itself purring against her skirts, the firelight shining flames off its yellow eyes. "We all have gold in us, Master de Aurum." He flinched as she said his name, "some of us more than others. In some, it promotes a bright heart. In others, it heralds avarice. Gold attracts more gold. We both, you and I, have more than the usual share of gold inside us."

Despite his unease and his misgivings about her theories, de Aurum could not help but feel flattered.

"And I will pay you," he said, "When your charm has proved its worth."

Mother Pellar nodded. "As you will," she said.

✝

"A toast to Master Paignton and his damned brood, then!"

"And may they continue to receive their just rewards for their father's abominable slight of you, my good friend!"

Ale slopped across de Aurum's knuckles as his cup clashed with Finnemore's and his mouth stretched into a grin, manic with drink and disbelief at his luck. Around him, the inn seemed too loud, the candles too bright, the merriment on the faces which swam in and out of his vision too raucous. It was as if some terrible storm was brewing and unable to prevent it de Aurum must try to deny it. Finnemore said, "A toast to you, too, Walt, and to your Anne and young Henry both — may your fortunes be as blessed as Paignton's are cursed!"

"Dear Kit, no talk of curses, please."

The words tumbled out unbidden and de Aurum winced to hear Finnemore's delighted laughter.

"What, superstitious, Walt? I daresay you think that old maid's cunning charm hidden in Paignton's bushes did the trick. Does this mean you'll now be parting with those six crowns she tried to swindle you of?" Finnemore winked, brandishing his half-drained cup.

De Aurum forced his grin back on display. He felt unusually light-headed. He said, loudly, "Maybe it did, maybe not—but I'll not be parting with any coin for a bottle of vinegar piss from as rank a witch as ever rode on ragwort."

Finnemore nodded over de Aurum's shoulder, gesturing with his cup, his eyes still alight with amusement.

"Then you can tell her that yourself."

"Kit, really—" de Aurum started to say, then he felt it: the volume of conversation dipped almost imperceptibly; the patrons crowded around tables drew so slightly away from the entrance of the place as to only be noticeable en masse as a vague but palpable discomfiture.

Turning around in his chair, de Aurum could see at first only the proprietor, hanging his head in an attitude of shame. Then he spotted the reason for the publican's apologetic stance heading towards him through the crowded room; a hobbling black figure with one hand raised.

"Walter de Aurum."

The irrational panic that de Aurum felt, he could not betray to the room at large. Bad enough that she had disrespected him when he visited her home; to now intimidate her way, probably by means of empty threats, into a gentleman's drinking establishment and confront him in public was unheard-of. Superstitious fear warred with indignant bravado. He half-rose in his seat.

"Do not stand, I will sit."

"You most certainly will not. Who let you in here?"

Mother Pellar raised her eyebrows, which were long and wispy at their peaks, like goose down. She said, "Why, the kind publican let me in, for to collect my debt from you, sir. And in order that I didn't turn his wine sour." She smiled; the movement of her mouth raising the edge of her veil a little, the ripples stretching to the corners of her eyes.

"Well, unlike our gullible publican, I am not moved by your hollow bluffs, so you'd best be on your way."

"Pardon me, Master de Aurum, but I make no bluffs. All I wish is simply to be paid that which I'm owed for a service rendered and then I'll be on my way. It is your choice."

"And what choice might that be?"

Around him the room poised, listening intently to his humiliating exchange. There *was* no choice. He could not back down.

Leaning close and lowering her voice so that only de Aurum could catch the words, Mother Pellar said "Pay me my gold or that curse which you have wished upon your rival will be returned threefold upon you."

De Aurum's mouth twitched. Wrapping his hand around his almost empty cup, he moved it in circles on the table top, following the grain of the wood. He said, "Your curses hold no water, old woman."

All around him it seemed like the whole room drew in a collective breath.

"Very well. Then in return for your treatment of me, a fly will cause your estate to fall."

De Aurum paused, taking in her words and a well of relief sprung inside him. A chuckle shook him, then stronger, until he was laughing out loud and joining the rest of the room in laughter, the tension broken.

"A fly?" De Aurum wiped his eyes on his cuff then shook the lace back into place, "A *fly* shall bring my walls down? Well, I shall afford you this — you certainly don't believe in making your task an easy one. Here," reaching into his purse he brought out a couple of coins, which he offered to Mother Pellar, "a penny for your lucky charm and one more for entertaining us so well today. Now, we are even."

Looking from his outstretched hand to his eyes, Mother Pellar made no move to take the money. Her skirts edged empty stools aside as she turned and wove her way out of the inn.

"It's a rank old witch, indeed," said Finnemore, slapping de Aurum reassuringly on the shoulder. But he said it quite after Mother Pellar had left the room.

✝

"They say she can see the future."

"*Could* see the future, you mean," Henry de Aurum said, "tell me, did she predict this do you think?" He frowned at the momentary golden blinding as he raised his arm holding his lantern higher, the beam dazzling in the darkened and empty street which returned the sound of their footsteps. Beside him, his companion shivered and drew his cloak tighter about him.

"Are you not troubled at all by her reputation?"

De Aurum snorted, his eyes still fixed ahead at their destination.

"Her reputation? Reputation as an old fraud and trickster!"

"But Henry, your father…"

De Aurum paused, the lantern swinging from its ring, sending devils of shadow capering across the walls of the nearby houses.

"My father, precisely: my father whom she brought to ruin with her manipulation. Do you know, Will, that on his deathbed he asked me to right this so-called curse that has been visited upon our family?"

"Right it? But how? Mother Pellar is dead."

At these words Will shivered again, perhaps not only from the unseasonable cold, as they neared the cottage at the end of the street. De Aurum said, "He wished me to pay her six gold crowns, for a spell she cast for him when I was but a child. He told me that she had a love of gold, that she said that everyone has gold inside them—"

"Inside them?"

"A metaphor, Will, a mere mawkish symbol of man's spiritual worth."

"So you believe none of it? What of Master Flye?"

De Aurum looked at Will, the lamplight turning his face to a flickering skull, his eyes dark hollows.

"None of it. When Paignton's damned crony attacked my father's house, it was nothing more than coincidence. Master Flye! That Flye was as superstitious a fool as my poor father was reduced to, to believe rumours of a curse were grounds enough to challenge his friend's alleged *persecutor.* " De Aurum placed his lantern down on a wall of waist-height, bordering the now-untended garden of the last cottage on the street, and wiped his hands on the skirts of his coat. "No, it was our family who were persecuted, by that old witch who lived here. Pay her a visit he told me, so pay her a visit I will—but I'll no more give up any more of our family's estate to her than I will believe in her godless conjuring."

They had been quite prepared to force the door, but in the event they didn't have to. The front door of the cottage swung open on ruined hinges, with a noise like a fox's bark. Inside was silent, the fire dead and cold, the only light source the lantern which de Aurum now trained upon the parlour.

It was hard to tell, without seeing the place prior to its owner's demise, what if anything had been taken, but the room in which they stood certainly looked bare—no kettle in the fireplace or candles on the mantel. All that remained was furniture; a heavy oak table and a rocking chair. These were both covered in a thick layer of dust, for all around the room the lantern light revealed plaster torn from the walls, the bare wooden laths showing through like bones. De Aurum said, "So much for her reputation. You see, Will, it is a modern age—men desire wealth more than they fear magic."

Will nodded, but he was looking at the table, on which a large, black-bound book lay, untouched.

"She's not here though."

"There's another room," De Aurum inclined his head towards the connecting door. The boards creaked under his boot heels as he approached. The door exuded, somehow, a notion of contained menace, brooding and indefinable. When de Aurum flung it open, Will jumped back with a yell and he himself flinched as a black cloud enveloped them both and a piercing shriek sounded.

"Flies, man, merely insects!"

Raising the lantern, de Aurum showed the cloud dissipate as quickly as it had appeared. Near to the floor another shriek sounded and then a rising hiss. Onto the table a tabby cat jumped, the lamplight picking out each raised hackle as it arched its back and spat. Will lowered the arm he'd flung up to protect his face.

"Just a cat."

Pacing around the black tome on the table, the cat glowered. When Will took a step towards it, it jumped from the table and streaked out through the open front door into the street.

They turned their attention back towards the second room. It seemed darker, if possible, than the main room, although how when both were equally ill-lit was a mystery. Perhaps because this sleeping chamber was smaller, the walls seeming to crouch in around them like a circle of great dark creatures bending down to look. There was plaster off the walls here, too, lending the small space the feel of being inside a ribcage, their twin life essence in the dead house an incongruous heart, beating after death. But the room was not quite so ransacked as the first and the probable reason for that was laid out upon the bed.

"There she is," said Will, his voice little more than a whisper.

Swaddled still in her long black garments, Mother Pellar presented a very small figure indeed. Only her knotted white hands crossed upon her chest and the upper part of her face showed pale in the lamplight. Despite her stature and even in death, she was imposing: the darkness of her black-clad form seemed to hold weight that belied her size and the light flickering on her closed eyelids seemed to show them twitching, like in dreaming sleep. After a moment, de Aurum handed the lantern to Will and bent closer, studying.

"There she is indeed. Not so terrifying now, I deem." He reached down a hand and then paused, waving away a lingering few flies that still buzzed around the corpse. "I always wondered, from my father's tales, why she wore a veil. Now we shall see."

Will did not just avert his eyes but turned bodily away from the scene and even de Aurum would have had to acknowledge a slight trepidation over what he was about to witness, as the light dimmed a little with Will's retreat. But flipping up the thin muslin, so that it instead covered the old woman's closed eyes, no terrible deformity or otherwise hideous visage was revealed more than lips slightly shrunken and pulled back in death's grimace.

De Aurum began to laugh. He laughed as if he couldn't stop and the harsh sound was terrible in the funeral stillness of the room.

"We all have gold inside us, Will. Look here," At this, Will turned, reluctantly, "here was her hidden fortune: a cunning woman indeed." And the light chimed off the bright row of Mother Pellar's top teeth: six crowns of gold. "Here, Will, bring that light closer."

"Why, what would you do?"

De Aurum beckoned. The lantern illuminated only the bed at such close quarters, a ghastly boat afloat in a sea of night. De Aurum, twitched back his coat sleeves and waved aside another fly. He said, "I would claim compensation for the ruin inflicted on my family."

Taking her front teeth firmly between finger and thumb, de Aurum pulled. As they came loose, he swatted away a final fly that had lit upon the back of his hand just long enough for him to feel the sting of its bite.

✝

Die Booth lives in Chester, UK and enjoys tea, old things and goth music. When not exploring abandoned places Die writes speculative fiction for places like Litro and The Fiction Desk. Currently editing a novel entitled 'Embedded', Die has recently co-edited the Re-Vamp *anthology and has stories due out in anthologies* Fear, Bloody Fabulous *and* The Art of Fairytales. *You can visit Die at* http://diebooth.wordpress.com/

Lecherous

MARTEN HOYLE

The lifestyle of the promiscuous is something I have long viewed as a game akin to Russian Roulette. To leap between the sheets with a total stranger for anonymous passion, protected or not, is like placing a gun against one's temple and hoping upon pulling the trigger that no bullet will pierce the skull. Of course, in this case, the bullets are diseases; the majority of them incurable. I dread such things as embarrassing clusters of warts, incarnadined eruptions of chancroid, foul-scented secretions of the urethra and (let us not forget) the terrifying immunological disorders with the same trepidation an arachnophobic sort feels upon encountering a spider, or the acrophobic man feels when facing a prodigious height. And yet, I blush to confess it, there was a period in my own history wherein I led a shamelessly licentious existence, seeking to fill a void I felt in my soul with the touch of nameless men. Something about placing the metaphoric gun to my head thrilled me, made me quiver with euphoria. I was a daredevil of the flush. I adored the danger, and I placed myself in harm's way often. Worse however than any disease known to man was the bullet I nearly fired.

We live in an age of superficiality—an age where relationships are built through the profiles we make of ourselves on the internet. It seems the days my father often speaks of whilst complaining about the current state of the world; days when men and women became acquainted in reality and established such things as trust and care, are gone—or at least fading away. Our idea of companionship is sharing links in a chat window or "liking" the thoughts our electronic "friends" display. And we meet our lovers there, in that pseudo-realm.

All connections, whether they were dating sights or "social" networks were my hunting ground; some men rejected me, most did not. As I have said, there was a void in my soul; a void which I felt I could fill with the touch of another human presence.

The websites acted as a lubricant for my tongue, somehow giving me the ability to skip all the formalities I would employ upon meeting a stranger face-to-face. I could jump straight in with both feet by giving immediate praise for good looks and masculinity accompanied by graphic descriptions of all I wished to do to their bodies. Both of us (no doubt) lying about being tested for HIV; exchanging pictures of my penis in exchange for one of their own; sealing the deal by obtaining an address and being given a time to arrive at every lecherous tryst.

I was a fool.

Pure and simple. But with no friends apart from the bylines and colorful syntax of old books, the ghosts of classical composers and the fine strokes of ancient art, I was lonely and wretched. I saw no pleasant alternative to meeting people, such as an awkward and drunken prelude to the establishment of such things as boundaries and *imaginable*, (but never *probable*) *eventual* friendship in a bar.

So, on a lonesome night in December, I searched the usual websites for a Romeo. After a few hours of fruitless coquetting, I came across the profile of a user who caught my eye. He was a handsome man in his late thirties with short black hair, a pair of gorgeous brown eyes looking out from above a perfect smile of pearly teeth and deep, adorable dimples. His pose and his smile seemed forced to me; he exhibited himself to show off his athletic form, shirtless and with his hands behind his head. Forced though it may be, the physique matched my taste with its muscular abdomen and protruding, spider web network of veins on the flexed biceps. He wore blue jeans, lightly faded and low enough to reveal his pubic region, which was shaved and inviting.

Abandoning, as I always did, the voice with which I generally write so as not to intimidate or repel him, I sent him the simplest message: "You're hot" and gave him my name.

He replied quickly with his own name, Jamal, and said he thought I was hot as well.

Confident that I had found someone, I asked where he lived and was surprised to find he resided right here in Spokane. Usually, I had to drive all the way to the surrounding towns like Medical Lake or Cheney to meet my partners. Here was one only a few miles away from my apartment. I crossed my fingers and hoped for an engagement.

We exchanged a few more messages, asking each other the common questions: Top or bottom, cut or uncut, what size, etc. Then we swapped pictures of our members. When I saw the size of his, my mouth watered. I wanted him and I said so. He replied with his address and an invitation.

He lived alone (so I thought) and he lived comfortably on a substantial salary in a two-story house built in the Victorian style, painted sky-blue with bay windows framed in Romanesque columns. The patio, which encompassed the whole domicile, was free of snow; decorated with flower pots whose blooms had wilted in the frigid temperature. Three stone steps led to the front door and the bell rang the *Westminster Chimes*; the interior of the house was lavish. Upon entering I saw one opening which led to the living room with its oak furniture, TV equipped with the latest gaming systems, cuckoo clock and family photos framed above the brick mantelpiece and a stereo which was a three-in-one CD, cassette and record player. Ahead, the hall led to the pinewood floor, white walls decorated by painted columns of buttery flowers, and the matching pinewood table and chairs of the kitchen. To my right, there was a carpeted stairway.

A peculiar odor greeted me; something musty that I couldn't quite put my finger on; a fume which disturbed the overall atmosphere of the place, making it unpleasant despite its beauty. Mingled with the perfume of incense and aroma therapy candles the spoor was all the more oppressive. It was like the redolence of a bathroom when sprayed with a scented air freshener after a repugnant excretion; it does not mask the odor of feces but makes the room stink of feces mixed with strawberries or whatever essence.

Not wanting to be rude, I didn't mention or give any sign that I noticed the stench, but Jamal, after closing the door behind me said he hoped I didn't mind it and explained that he had only recently moved into the house and that the carpets needed to be replaced. I lied that I hardly noticed.

He guided me to the living room and told me to make myself comfortable while he poured wine.

"I like a glass before..." he grinned. "*You know.*"

"So do I," I lied. I preferred just to get into the place of my lovers, do my business and then leave with no questions asked. But, again not wanting to be rude, I sat on the sofa, dealt with the smell and waited patiently for my host to return. During his absence, I surveyed the carpet and honestly couldn't find anything wrong with it. It was white as the snow outside with absolutely no stain in sight.

He came back a few minutes later with two glasses filled to the brim, carrying them carefully so as not to spill.

"I hope you like red," he said as he sat next to me and placed the glasses on his coffee table.

"My favorite," I said, hoping we would drain our glasses quickly and hurry to his bedroom.

He raised his glass.

"Cheers," he said.

I lifted mine to his and took a great gulp which promptly warmed my stomach and filled me with a good, buzzing sensation as if my nerves were being tickled.

"That's very good," I said.

"The finest," he boasted.

I took another drink, and when I placed the glass back on the table, I nearly dropped it and soiled his carpet. The warmth which filled me felt suddenly heavy. My heart slammed against my ribcage with a breath so long between each beat that I swore for a moment it would stop and I would drop dead. My head thickened, felt framed by a dense fog that crept into my skull and flooded my brain. I swooned.

Oh, God! He drugged me!

"Are you alright?" he asked. His voice seemed to come to me from a great distance, from another world. I rose and attempted to run, but my legs felt like water and gave out beneath me. I fell into the table, spilling the wine. In desperation, I rolled off the surface and my head kissed the floor. I tried to raise myself onto my hands and knees, to *crawl* from him. But my limbs refused to work; my will to survive gave me a feeling of strength like I have never known before, but my arms and legs felt disconnected from my body, unable to take the frantic messages from my brain to *move*.

Helpless, I fought with myself, trying in vain to keep my eyes open. But the world was spinning and my head was so lost in that drugged haze that it felt good to close my eyes and let the darkness be my only sight. And I sensed myself sinking into the Cimmerian shade as if the floor had turned to quicksand and was sucking me downward. I heard myself utter a single, labored entreaty of, "Please...don't..." and then, I knew nothing; I felt nothing. I left the world behind.

✝

I woke, expecting to find myself restrained by a cuff and chain, but to my surprise I saw the ceiling of the living room and Jamal's face hovering over me.

"Are you okay?" he asked.

"I..." I didn't know what to say.

"You were out for a good ten minutes," he said. "Was the wine *that* strong?"

"I..."

"You..."

"I thought you drugged me."

He frowned. "Drugged you?" he said. "Why would I do that? Look...if you want to go home, I understand. You probably should."

"No," I said. "No. I want to stay."

He smiled.

"Come with me," he said. "I'll take care of you."

Taking me by the hand, he helped me get back onto my feet and led me up the stairs and into the bedroom.

I needn't tell you what happened. It was amazing; I felt truly connected to him. Just like all the others. For a time, the hole inside of me was filled. When we were finished, I made ready to say the usual, "Well, I have to go," followed by whatever excuse I could make on the spot, but I was utterly exhausted. When I rolled off of him onto my back, I fell instantly to sleep.

I wish to note now that we made love with the lights off. I did not see the symbol on his stomach, which he did not bear in the photo on the dating sight. The picture, I believe, was taken before he came to the house.

✝

I woke at dawn. Sniffing, I became at once aware of the smell from the night before, worse than before as if the source was within close proximity. It gagged me.

I brought myself to a sitting position and looked to the body beside me. With a scream, I leapt from the bed and made for the door, but was arrested by the very thing I feared the night before. I fell flat on my face, rose quickly and found that my foot was cuffed in iron, attached to a chain fastened into the wall. Trying in vain to pull my foot through the manacle and escape from the thing which lay on the bed, I fell a second time and crawled in a frenzy toward the door.

Desiccated, naked, prostrate with mouth agape and grey bones exposed through colorless rags of what once was flesh, a carcass lay where Jamal had been when I fell asleep. Looking at it over my shoulder as I attempted to reach the door, I opened my mouth to cry for help, but vomited instead, and then collapsed.

At length, with my throat burning, my stomach quivering and nerves tingling on edge, I succeeded in rising to my knees and screaming, "HELP! SOMEONE HELP!"

I heard footsteps on the stairs and screamed louder, louder for someone, *anyone* to call the police, to save me.

The door opened. It was not Jamal who entered, but an elderly man wearing a three-piece suit. In one hand, he held a strange, metal object like a mask suspended from a leather belt. In the other, he held a branding iron with a stamp that glowed crimson.

"Good morning, sir," he said.

I am not by any means a violent man. I have never been in a fight in my life. But when I saw that iron, I prepared to strike.

"You think you're going to burn me with that?" I said leaping to my feet and raising my fists in a way which looked comical to the stranger, for he laughed at me.

"I don't think you'll have much choice," he said.

He stepped aside, making way. Into the room, three men dashed on me with such speed that I had no time to react or defend myself. In the next instant, I was on the floor with my arms and legs pinned down. I struggled, but I could not break free.

The stranger in the suit joined his cohorts and knelt beside me. Laying the iron next to him, he placed the metal mask over my mouth and nose. He then buckled the leather belt tightly round my head and locked it into position. After this, he took the iron back into his hand.

"This is going to be very unpleasant for you," he said.

I screamed, but my voice hardly pierced the mask. A muffled bellow reached my ears and, without warning, I started to cry. I was going to die here, of that I was sure. I had entered a house occupied, I assumed (judging from the inverted cross of the stamp that the old man raised) by a Satanic cult.

Pain that was beyond pain struck me when at last he pressed the brand down on my stomach. I shrieked, I kicked my legs and tried to lift my arms, to grasp the rod and free myself of it, but the men held me firm in their grasp. I could not smell it, but I could see the smoke rising as my skin and fat cells melted and effervesced beneath the decalescent symbol.

Once he decided I had been tortured enough for the time being, the old man backed away and ordered the three to release me. At once, I grasped my stomach and curled into the fetal position. I wanted to die, the agony was so excruciating that below the mask I told them to kill me, please kill me. And for a blissful moment, I believed I *was* dying, for I felt consciousness slipping away and when I passed out, I prayed that the blackness I welcomed was the void of eternal rest.

When I came to, the old man was crouching before me. My wound screamed with undulations of fiery misery that flowed throughout my body. To make matters worse, my tormentor was touching me, rubbing my mutilation with his spidery fingers, which I saw were coated in an iridescent, greasy substance.

"I am sorry, sir," he said. "I thought you were a day walker like me. Like *us*." He corrected himself, referring (no doubt) to his thugs.

"What are you...talking about?" I tried to speak, but only emitted inaudible groans through the mask.

"But I can see," he said, raising his free hand; in it, he held the condom I wore the night before; "I was greatly mistaken. I *do* beg your forgiveness."

"Fuck you," I wished he could hear me.

"I will leave you to Jamal," he said and, letting the condom fall to the floor, he took from his pocket a small, brass key. Standing, he walked to the bed and laid the key on the nightstand, next to the corpse. Then, without another word, he left and closed the door behind him.

The moment he left, I rose and plunged onto the mattress, and reached over the carcass for the key. The nightstand was mere inches from my fingertips, but the chain held me back. I again tried to pull my foot out of the cuff, but managed only to cut myself. Despairing, not knowing what Jamal would do to me whenever he returned, I sank back to the ground and lay weeping for hours.

Around...I do not know what time, the door opened and one of the thugs entered with a plate of food—scraps, really. There was a drumstick with barely a mouthful of meat on the bone, a few peas and a small white mass of rice. He set this on the floor in front of me and from a scabbard he wore withdrew a dagger with a curved blade like a steel smile. He waved the weapon before my eyes and tapped my mask with its tip.

"Now," he said. "If I take that mask off, are you going to scream?"

Although I wanted to die, I decided to cooperate. In my mind, I saw him sticking the dagger into my stomach and I thought of the suffering I might endure as I bled to death. If only a painless demise would present itself.

Closing my eyes, I nodded. The man nodded back and, leaving me for a moment took the key from the nightstand and unfastened the lock of the binding leather. I once more breathed the stagnant, repulsive fragrance of death, but it was a relief to smell *anything* other than the cold metal of the mask.

"Eat," the man ordered.

Truly, I was not hungry. I doubted if I could ever eat again, but I didn't want to anger my imprisoner. So with great difficulty, I ate what was given me and when the plate was empty, the man put the mask on me again.

"You know," he said after returning the key to the night table, "I thought you were one of us this morning, too." He kneeled in front of me. "Honestly, I don't know why Jamal spared you. The wine *was* drugged, but at the last second, he hesitated. I wonder what he sees in you."

Without warning, he set the blade against my arm and slit me open. I winced, for the sensation was both fiery and icy and sent a shiver through my frame.

"All I see is scum," he said and, for no reason, slashed my cheek. I felt tears stinging my eyes. He was going to butcher me. I knew it. This was the end; a long and painful end.

He leaned forward so that his lips hung over the fresh wound; I felt his breath hot against my skin. Then, so repulsive, he extended his tongue and licked the blood from my face.

"No," he said. "I don't see anything special."

He rose and, sheathing his knife said, "It's getting dark outside;" and on his way out told me, "Don't worry; it'll be over soon."

And he closed the door.

Once alone, I looked out the window. He was right. The day was getting dark. I must have passed out at several points throughout the day. There are periods—hours, which are an utter blur to me; periods of indistinguishable blends of images and shadow that if I try to think about hurt my head. It was when the sun went down that I woke from one such period and heard the soft footsteps. I asked, trying to see through the absolute darkness, "Who's there?"

"Are you awake?" a familiar voice asked.

"Yes."

Jamal turned on the light. I shut my eyes under the glare; opened them, closed them, opened them, closed them until they adjusted themselves to the light.

"You really should have left last night."

I looked in the direction of his voice and prayed while I screamed that I was dreaming. Not this! Anything but this!

Standing by the door, still desiccated, but *changing,* gaining color, muscle, throbbing blue veins and a heart that beat beneath the exposed ribs was the carcass I woke next to.

Jamal knelt before me and showed me something he held in his hand. The key.

"Don't scream," he said. Even as he spoke, fibrous formations of flesh wound themselves swiftly together over his bones, restoring the beauty which had so sparked my Lobito the previous evening.

"I am a Night Walker," he said as he placed the key into the latch of the cuff; "The only one in this house. I have life only when the world is dark."

He released my foot and then, he unlocked the mask.

"It's lucky for you that you used a condom," he said. "Otherwise —"

I didn't give him a chance to explain anything to me. With what strength I had, I shoved him away from me and, leaving my clothes on the floor ran out into the hall and down the stairs. On the way down, I chanced to look into the living room and there beheld four shrunken, grey corpses one of which wore a three-piece suit.

Day Walkers.

"This is only a dream," I told myself.

Yes! It was only a dream. Thinking thus, the whole ordeal seemed ludicrous. So ludicrous that I laughed as I descended, threw open the door and ran out into the December night. It was only a dream; I would waken at any moment. I laughed naked in the snow, I laughed naked in my car and I laughed all the way home, and when I was at last safe in my own apartment, well, I laughed then, too.

At length, my laughter turned to tears. I was in the shower, crouching and cradling myself, hugging my knees against my breast and rocking.

For years, I have kept the encounter with this terror a secret. I share it now because I am, in a way, glad it happened. Today, I am thankful to be alive and thankful to have left my lecherous phase behind me.

✝

Having taught himself to write at the age of ten, **Marten Hoyle** *grew into a struggle throughout his teenage years to accept his own sexual identity and turned to writing for help. Today, Hoyle composes tales for the therapeutic purpose of self relief. He lives in Spokane, Washington.*

The Corpse Road

CHRISTIAN A. LARSEN

Western Arkansas was always an odd place. It wasn't quite desert, but it was sliding that way. And it had always been sliding that way as far back as white men could remember—or red men, for that matter. The ground wasn't so much soil anymore as it was chipped shale, and the only green was in the needles on the pine trees. It was the kind of country that pretends at being good land, only because what's to the west was so goddamned bleak and bone-bleaching. Oh, it could get hot there, too, especially come August, when the bees crawled around drunk from the simmering heat and even the hummingbirds forgot their tune, but it was never hellish like it was out west.

Western Arkansas was more like purgatory, even in the shade of the creaking pines that bent and swayed in the dry wind like the bones of old men.

But something had crept into the landscape that wasn't there before.

Judson sat on the edge of the porch and looked west, holding his arm over his eyes to keep the sun out, but he wasn't sweating—not anymore.

He didn't know if the legends about Charon the Boatmen were true, but if they were, he was it. He'd seen a lot of folks pass by, a lot of men, during the war years, heading west like they were escaping something, the violence, maybe. Or maybe themselves. But he knew what West meant. West meant the end of the road. The Corpse Road. And that's why he sat down on the storefront porch and just looked that way, getting as used to the heat as best he could. He might have been there years. Or maybe days. Time was hard to tell along the Corpse Road.

The funny thing was, he seemed to be the only person who could tell the way things really were, and not just in bits and pieces. Everyone else just kept sidling on by, with holes blown in their faces from mortar shots, or limbs ripped from their sockets by cannonball fire, and they would still be talking about what really did them in — what put them on this road instead of the other. And they had a way of selling it. One soldier with a blood soaked coat walking shoulder to shoulder with another kept talking about "a round little bundle on top of two spindly legs." It made the other one grin so wide he had to keep popping his jaw back into his skull. His teeth looked like the edge of a saw, almost silver in the hot August sun. *Could've been silver the way they gleamed through the rip in his cheek,* Judson supposed. Sawtooth stopped smiling when the soldier with the blood-soaked coat started talking about what he would do to split that little bundle like a cord of wood.

"You stop talking that way, Horatio Demby." When he said 'stop' and 'Horatio,' the gash in his cheek flapped and he sounded a little like a duck.

"Easy, Pard," said Demby. "What's wrong in appreciating a slice of fruit, even if it's not on your plate?"

And what he added made Judson feel like blushing, and he may have, but he didn't know if he was in a position to blush anymore. The nearest mirror was in the store behind him, but he didn't want to look in that mirror again, anyway. Not so soon. He didn't much care for what his recent turn of events had done for his appearance. And then he wondered how recent those events were, because — as he had remarked to himself more than once — time was hard to figure along the Corpse Road.

As he was pondering this, the two men, Demby and Sawtooth, took to blows. Judson could never be sure that Sawtooth struck first, but it sure seemed the likeliest thing. Even from his place on the porch, he could see how the man with the ripped cheek had carried tension in his shoulders, a sure sign that a fight was brewing. Some people just had a knack for avoiding trouble, and Judson was one of them. He never was caught in a fight he didn't enter willingly, because that tension — the one Sawtooth had been carrying — was like an electrical storm. It literally used to raise Judson's hackles when he felt it. It felt the same way now, but if he wasn't sure if he could blush, he was equally unconvinced about his hackles' ability to rise up. Sometimes it was just better to sit on the porch and feel time slide on by. Or imagine it was sliding. Because Judson thought sometimes that time just wasn't moving at all, not where he was.

Sawtooth hit Demby. Hard. He knocked him to the road with his fist, and dust puffed up like dragon smoke. He followed that up with a kick to the chest, and Judson could hear the sticky sound that Sawtooth's foot made as it hit bullseye in the middle of that dark stain. His boot came back covered in what looked like tar, thick and choking, and he kicked Demby again, this time in the face. "You're a sick bastard, talking about young ladies like that! I'll kill you for it!" His jaw unbuttoned from his face again, the dry muscles in his cheek pulling back in a grimace that looked an awful lot like a smile.

Judson wasn't sure if Sawtooth was speaking figuratively, or if he even realized they were dead. The Corpse Road was no place for the living.

Sawtooth snapped his jaw back into place and swirled his boot in the dirt, bringing up another cloud of dust, the way a baseball manager might do to home plate after he was already ejected by the umpire. But that was his mistake, because the fight wasn't over—not by a long shot. Demby lashed out with his hands and dragged Sawtooth to the ground and climbed on top of him. He wasn't punching, though. He was clawing. Squeezing. It reminded Judson of what Demby wanted to do to the round little bundle on top of those two spindly legs. And when Demby climbed up to Sawtooth's face, he reached over the top of his head and started peeling his cheek up toward his hairline. What came off looked like leather. There wasn't much blood, but there were blood-curdling screams.

So the dead still know pain, thought Judson as he watched Sawtooth's skull emerge from his own face while Demby pulled and pulled like a madman.

Judson went inside the store to get away from the ripping screams. Yet something else drove him inside. That noise he couldn't quite place that had crept into the landscape. Even if he wasn't in Western Arkansas, he'd been here plenty long, and he'd never heard this noise before. He stopped at the counter, rifling through a bucket of penny candy. He didn't want to eat any. He tried eating some candy when he first got here, years…days ago, and it tasted like nothing. Not a thing. He was moving his hand around in the bucket because he wanted to cover up that noise, the one he had never heard before.

There were no lights on in the general store, and the windows were shuttered, but Judson could still see. He didn't know electric lights, but somehow because some of the passersby on the Corpse Road knew them, Judson did, too. He supposed that the light was something like that, but he didn't see any bulbs, and the color was wrong. Either he was imagining the light entirely, or it was the spook-light coming from the marsh near his home in Macon County. And that was a long way away. Long time, too. Or maybe it was just a few days. Time was hard to tell along the Corpse Road.

And maybe that was because there was no one to pass the time with. Everybody Judson saw shambling on by never slowed down, even with injuries that would have laid a man low—or killed him. Legs frayed open like green tree branches, but dry, all their bleeding done. Or holes poked through skulls so damned big you could see daylight through them. But that wasn't why they were heading West, where the sun burned hotter still. They were heading West because they weren't good enough for the East. And while that conjured up images in Judson's mind of New York and Philadelphia, he knew that's not really what 'Back East' meant. Back East meant, as the preacher man put it, 'Great Reward.'

Judson died fighting for the Union in the Battle of Jenkins Ferry. The date was April 30, 1864. The Confederates were running them down after Major General Frederick Steele's forces lost at Poison Springs. The Union forces were just trying to cross the Saline River so they could regroup at Little Rock, but they were caught by the tail, and a few hundred men lost their lives on both sides. Judson had been gutshot, and remembering that, he looked down at his own coat. It looked like Demby's, with a dark stain spread across it.

That's when the walking started. Something like a thousand men that day just got up and started walking. Half went East and half went West. Both groups had a mix of Blue and Grey, so Providence didn't seem to have a rooting interest in the War Between the States, at least not from the look of things. Judson marched West, and like most of them, he supposed, he wanted to turn right back around but found that he couldn't. It wasn't so much fighting the urge, as the urge was fighting him. He just couldn't turn around. There was a force at work stronger than gravity.

One young man, a Confederate volunteer by the name of Reynolds who wasn't much more than a boy—he did try to march East. Reynolds had mentioned how much nicer they were going to have it over there, and Judson knew he was right. He knew it without knowing, but that didn't change the knowing. Back East was going to be absolutely wonderful, but out West? That was going to be one hard row to hoe. Everybody on the Corpse Road knew it, but they just kept on with the march, like salmon at mating season. Because they couldn't help it.

Reynolds stopped, the dust settling around his boots like silt. The westering sun was shining on the boy as big and round as frying pan, burning white hot with the long shadows of the late afternoon everywhere but on him. He did an about face, like he was trained by his drill sergeant when talk of fighting in the war was all glorious and good, and he hadn't seen anyone holding their guts in with their hands, or begging a field surgeon not to cut off their leg. In the East, the sky was cool and dark, but starry with a slice of moon like a picnic pie. He leaned into the East like a wind was blowing, but there was no wind. Something was holding him up, either pushing from the East, or pulling from the West. Judson never did figure that one out.

The boy started in on his hip-deep winter march, picking up first one foot and then the other, lifting each boot like it was made of lead. He managed a couple of steps, too, which was a goddamned miracle.

And then his flesh started peeling off, at first in tiny threads, then in ribbons, and finally in whole sheets the size of a kerchief or bigger. Reynolds tried turning West again, but it was too late for that. Whatever power was compelling them was through forgiving them, at least on the Corpse Road, because the last Judson saw of the Reynolds kid was blowing West on a hot breeze with an echoing scream, quicker than any of the rest. Fighting it just brought it all on faster and in the worst possible way.

"Judson Campbell, is that you?" one of his fellow marchers asked.

"Getting hard to recognize, now that my blood's let?"

"I s'pect we all are."

Judson couldn't argue. 'Ashen-faced' didn't quite hit the mark. Billy Ogden, the voice, anyway, speaking with him, if not the face, looked like he was made out of clay, the kind that's used to having water running over it, keeping it smooth and wet. But Billy's clay face didn't have water running over it anymore; the water was gone, and the sun baked his flesh dry so it cracked in a thousand tiny wounds at the corners of his mouth, his sunken eyes, and in the creases around his nose. If there had been blood, it would have been a mess. But they were all dry and dead, and Ogden's tendons creaked like leather thongs when he talked.

"You know where we're headed?" asked Ogden.

Judson shrugged. "Wouldn't hurt to speak it now, I guess," he said. "I think we're going to Hell."

"Whatever the case, it's been an awful long haul so far." A fat bluebottle crawled fly out of Ogden's mouth and buzzed slowly away.

"And I'd always been told war and hell were next door neighbors."

"I'm serious, Jud," said Ogden. "I don't think I'm up for this."

"You think a good night's rest will bring back your vim?" asked Judson, forcing a smile. It felt like a crack right across his face. Maybe it was. "We can't go East. I've seen what happens if you try. And anyway, it's like there's a hunk of pig iron in me, and there's a lodestone just past sunset. Can't go back East."

"Who said anything about back East?" asked Ogden, slowing down a little. "I don't want to go back. I'm just beat—dog tired. My feet feel like they're splitting in half inside m'boots. This is supposed to be our eternal rest. So why am I working so hard? I think I'll just rest here awhile. Find a creek to soak my feet."

"You've always been a shiftless bastard," said Judson. "How do you know you can even stop? That lodestone's something strong."

"Watch me."

Ogden laid down on the side of the road, stiff as a board with his hands folded over his stomach like he probably was on the banks of the Saline River after some Confederate ripped his leg open with a bayonet. He would have gotten away if he'd have been most other soldiers, but Ogden was always soft, taking twice as long to finish a task as anyone else, if he didn't try to pawn off the job on someone else. Judson was not sorry to see him disappear in the distance. He was tired of putting up with his nonsense.

But Ogden had stopped. That was the important thing. If Judson didn't want to go West, he didn't have to. He just couldn't go back East. So that's why he stopped at the general store. It was shady, dark, and quiet, and for someone in his condition, he figured that a place that was as quiet as the grave was a good fit. But it didn't stay that way, at least not when the Linville sisters stopped for a visit. The sun never went up or down—it just hung there—but being with those two felt like years, like Hell was nothing compared to them.

"Nettie, look, a shady spot," said one. She had a short haircut like someone cut off her ponytail with a bayonet, and a skimpy skirt that didn't much go past her hips. Her thighs would have been inviting if they weren't mottled grey with death, the blotches rising like a block of old, forgotten cheese. She could have been anywhere between eighteen and thirty-six, but whatever she was, she was long past her expiration, and so was her sister.

The other woman was more plump, or had been, but she had the same kind of bobbed haircut and a long feather boa draped around her shoulders. She was in equally bad shape as her sister, but her fishnet stockings and heavy rouge made the damage hard to read from a distance. "Maybe they've got some beauty cream in there," she croaked. "The sun is killing my skin. I'll be getting wrinkles soon."

The skinny one's name was Odelia. Judson just knew that somehow and for some God-forsaken reason, the word 'flapper' kept circling around in his head, but he didn't know what that meant. Or why Charleston was so important to them. They sure didn't talk like they were from South Carolina. They didn't even talk like they were ladies. At least, any ladies that Judson ever knew, except maybe the comfort women that followed the army around. They had mouths like sewers, and they sometimes smoked. The Linville sisters did, too. Or they used to. Odelia had a cigarette holder clenched between her teeth, but it was broken in half, just kind of dangling from her mouth. There was no sign of an actual cigarette, though.

Judson waved at them from the doorway, but they seemed to see right through him. But that wasn't exactly it. Nettie looked right past him, like he was in the way of the tinned food and dry goods behind the counter. When Odelia looked at him, he felt weighed, or measured in some way. Like he should have a price tag hanging from his nose — a white slave. But whatever price he would have fetched while he was drawing air, it was certainly less now. Hell, the tag might pull his nose off. As damaged as he was, though, it didn't stop Odelia from putting him on the scales in her mind, and he didn't like the feeling. Not one bit. He spoke to shake the moment.

"You ladies been on the road long?"

"Look at his old fashioned clothes," said Odelia, half giggling like someone half her age, or stewed on moonshine. Expensive, city moonshine, to be sure.

Nettie raised her chin to try to see over his shoulder. "Like a soldier."

"An old time soldier."

"I'll admit," said Judson, standing up straight in the doorway. "The uniform's seen a few hard miles. But it's current Union issue, or it was when it was handed to me. I'm not sure you could say the same about the skirts you're wearing. Or the boys' haircuts."

"Union issue?"

"You talk like our grandpa."

"What year is it?" asked Judson. "That you're from, I mean."

"It's 1925," answered Nettie.

"What kind of question is that?" asked Odelia.

By the time the Linville sisters had moved on, Odelia had emptied the cash register and taken whatever she thought was valuable in a gunny sack from behind the register, and Nettie had eaten empty half of the tins. Her dress looked like it was about to split. And so did her flesh, like an overcooked sausage. Or the dead soldiers that had been laying out in the sun too long after a battle but before the burials took place. Judson imagined he didn't look much better, but at least he didn't eat for the sake of it, or collect the valuables from a phantom general store out of greed. No, he was better than the Linville sisters. Better than the lot that had passed by. But they were all gone now. He hadn't seen anyone come by since Sawtooth and Demby. And that was years and years...or just minutes, ago.

But Judson wasn't alone.

He had that noise to keep him company.

The one that wasn't there before.

Judson shaded his eyes with his arm again. He wondered what kind of stink he was putting out that he couldn't smell. Even living, he could never smell his own stink, so he kept to a regular schedule for bathing just to make sure he wouldn't offend polite company. The war did that in, and then it did him in. An ignominious end to a noble gentleman. But the worst part was having to watch the trash walk on by on the Corpse Road. Body parts dropping off. Maggots in their ears, crawling around so much they almost made a sound. Those people all deserved what they got. Judson couldn't deny it. But what Providence was thinking to put him West instead of East, Judson could not get a true sounding. He was out of his depth.

Same with the sound.

It ate at him. It was the sound of regret. Not its own. His. Like locusts munching all the leaves off the trees in August when the sun was biggest, stripping everything bare so there was no where to hide from the light. And maybe that was what was happening, even though the trees were nothing but pine needles as far as he could see. Judson swallowed the knot in his throat. No spit. His Adam's Apple bobbed like a stone in a sock, all rough edges catching and unraveling everything they touched. He moved to wipe the sweat from his forehead and dusted off flakes of skin that had withered in the sun. He was a long time from sweating.

The sun beat down.

And the sound kept getting louder.

It sounded like God balling up wax paper in his hands, or maybe a forest fire, but there was no smoke, or it could have been drums, maybe drums, or a pack of wolves howling to beat the band. It sounded like all those things, and Judson knew it wasn't for him. He, the dutiful soldier, well-read, mother-and-country loving, who tithed every Sunday at church—and before the war, he was there every Sunday—he was not a part of that noise.

It was neither joyous nor mournful. It simply was. A force of nature. Or supernature, as the case may be.

But it was not for him.

And that's when he saw the first corpse walking East. They were the first successful eastbound steps anyone had taken in Judson's eyes since the day he died, and half the corpses headed toward Georgia or some such place. But the other thing, the odd thing, was that the body didn't look so corpse-like anymore. As it approached with more coming on behind, Judson watched the blotches of corpse blue shrink and disappear, like time working in reverse. It was a man, but not like any man Judson had ever known. His hips sashayed and his arms were thin and boyish, even womanish. And even grave-rumpled, Judson could see he took care with his hair. He was the kind of man that would have only survived in the city. Rent boys. That term was new to him, but somehow, he knew it. The man was obviously a gay cat.

"What's going on?" Judson asked, stepping off the porch. "How come you're headed East on the Corpse Road? And these other folks?"

"You haven't heard?" said the man in a soft, silky voice.

"Heard what?"

"The West is closed."

"Closed?"

"Done. They call it The Harrowing of Hell."

"Like in the Bible?"

Another person approached along the Corpse Road and came back to life. "Happened a long time ago. Or just now. But it doesn't really matter. The living see time as a string pulled straight. But it's really a wad of string, all knotted and crossed. It touches everywhere. It means nothing."

"What are you, a preacher or something?"

"No, I was a dry goods merchant. Ran a store like this, I guess."

Judson wanted to ask him more questions, but the merchant—like the gay cat before him—lost interest with the draw of the East pulling them on. It didn't matter, though. There were more people coming up the Corpse Road. In clumps of two or three now. And they were coming fast.

"Who's getting out?" Judson asked a group.

"Everyone," said a woman, the cruel lines in her face disappearing like the rot on her skin. "And we're getting new bodies. See?" She held out both of her arms to him like she was modeling new clothes.

"Everyone?" asked Judson, stepping on to the road to try to follow her. But when he tried to go East, filaments of skin started peeling away from his body and flying off on the updraft of a hot breeze. He stepped West again, rubbing his wounds, but the stinging wouldn't go away.

Crowds of people were coming along the Corpse Road, crowding the way east, but they all moved as one, and no one had to slow down. Every now and again, one or two of the people—they were no longer corpses, but living, people in the pink of health—would look at Judson, but they seemed to look right through him, and these were people that in life Judson would have looked at down his nose. All the way down. Queers, addicts, hogs, and abusers of the worst kind. But just like he knew rent boys and light bulbs well past his time, he knew another thought now. He knew that they had done their time while there was a chance. Now the West was closed. And the East, with its relief and reward, could never be his.

Ever.

Yet it had been his choice.

✝

Christian A. Larsen grew up in Park Ridge, Illinois and graduated from Maine South High School in 1993. He has worked as an English teacher, radio personality, newspaper reporter, and a printer's devil, and has been published by What Fears Become *(Imajin Books),* A Feast of Frights *(The Horror Zine Books),* The Ghost IS the Machine *(Post Mortem Press),* Fortune: Lost and Found *(Omnium Gatherum), and* Chiral Mad *(Written Backwards).*

Christian received his bachelor of science in broadcast journalism from the University of Illinois and studied secondary English education at National-Louis University. He lives with his wife and two sons in the fictional town of Northport, Illinois. Follow him on Twitter @exlibrislarsen or visit exlibrislarsen.com.

Deadweight

KEN MACGREGOR

Gregory Simmons was virtually awesome. Not so much in the real world, but his Avatar was: tall, handsome and grotesquely muscular; he could run and leap and fight and even fuck, if you knew the cheat codes. Gregory Simmons did, but he only used that particular cheat the one time, just to see. It was awkward, like walking in on your brother and his girlfriend. Other than satisfying his curiosity, though, he refused to use cheat codes. If you win without playing the game by the rules, what's the point? And Gregory Simmons was going to win. So far, he'd won every game he ever played. It was only a matter of time until be beat this one.

He was playing *Gods of Kromm*. His Avatar, Blackstone, had leveled up as high as he could go, but there were still four challenges he had yet to complete. Gregory made Blackstone jump up and down a few times and flex his biceps. A farm girl on the screen swooned; it was a nice touch. Gregory flipped screens to check vital stats; everything was perfect. His phone rang, but he didn't recognize the caller ID so he ignored it. It had been ringing a lot lately, but Gregory didn't want to talk to anyone. He wanted to win this damn game.

He picked up a piece of ham and pineapple pizza from the box, shook off the flies and reclaimed it as his own. He washed it down with a warm Coke; the kitchen and its fridge were just too far away. For a moment, Gregory looked around at his apartment in the real world. He saw the empty pizza boxes, Chinese food cartons and cans and cans of Coke and Mountain Dew. There were insects boldly wandering through the mess in the dim light coming through the blinds. As he watched, a large centipede crawled out of a soda can, its improbable number of legs twitching through the small opening. Gregory was repulsed, mostly by the bug, but also himself.

He shut out the real world and returned to the game. His Avatar was standing there, waiting for him patiently, occasionally tapping one foot or the other, looking around, shrugging or other small movements to keep the player from getting too bored.

"Okay, Blackstone," he said. "Let's do this thing." Gregory brought up the first of the four challenges and Blackstone tackled it with electronic vigor. It required both combat and strategy, which was the best kind; Blackstone rose to the occasion, a mighty warrior and Gregory's brain puzzled out the complicated riddles and they both moved past it. Three more and he could face the last Demon Lord at the end. He was pretty sure Blackstone would win that fight, and he was anxious to get to it.

Challenge number two was easier than the first: purely physical and no problem for Blackstone. Number three was mostly word games, tricky and damned time-consuming; after he finally puzzled them all out, he had to fight twenty-five Wargs at once.

That was awesome.

Gregory noted that three hours had passed, and that he had to pee. He had been putting it off for over an hour, but if he didn't go now, he was going to wet his pants. He peeled himself off the couch and lurched to the bathroom. He let fly and it lasted over a full minute, turning the water in the stained bowl a pale yellow. Gregory looked in the mirror. It had been weeks since he shaved, days since his last shower. He tried to remember the last time he'd brushed his teeth, but could not. He breathed into his hands and sniffed. Yuck. He looked at his dry toothbrush and the tube of Aim next to it. He stood like that for several seconds, pants still unbuttoned and tried to summon the energy to care.

Someone knocked on his door. He froze and stared at his reflection. Nobody visited him. Ever. The knock came again, louder. Gregory wondered if they could hear the background music of the game. He hoped not; he didn't want company. Didn't want to talk to anyone. They knocked again, pounding on the door.

"Hello? Is anyone there? We heard someone is still living here. You have to leave. You have to get out of there! This building has been condemned and will be torn down tomorrow! Hello?" There was a pause, then Gregory could hear muffled voices outside his door, then footsteps retreating.

Tearing down the building? That's insane. He'd lived here his whole life. He hadn't left his apartment in... months? A year? He couldn't remember. After the accident at work, he'd had no reason to go anywhere. Never having to work again was a small price to pay for one little toe. Come to think of it, he had noticed it was quiet lately. He couldn't remember the last time he heard old lady Smothers's TV being played too loudly. But, he figured she had died; she was, like a hundred and six or something. Maybe he was the only one there. Maybe they really were tearing down the building. Maybe he should have answered the door. But, they said it was happening tomorrow, so today was safe. He didn't have to leave yet. Gregory had plenty of time to finish his game.

Challenge number four was hard: Blackstone had to solve a puzzle, perform a difficult acrobatic feat *and* defeat a solid opponent. It took him nine attempts to pull it off. That was awesome. Gregory released the mouse and did a little victory dance with his fingers, the only part of him that ever moved fast. He was vaguely aware of noises outside and looked at the window. He could see the sky getting lighter behind the blinds. Was it morning already? He'd have to order breakfast soon; his stomach growled at the thought. After I beat this guy and win the game, Gregory decided. Then, I'll eat. Something else was nagging at him, too. Something about today. He couldn't remember.

On the screen, Blackstone faced the Demon Lord, drew his sword and shook his head, like *you ain't shit, buddy.* Gregory's left hand flew across the keys and his right manipulated the mouse. He was in the zone. He and Blackstone were wearing down the Demon Lord, but Blackstone was getting pretty beaten up, too. It was epic, perfect. The graphics were amazing: you could count the Demon Lord's teeth as he threatened to bite Blackstone's face off.

Gregory was peripherally aware of a large diesel engine firing up outside. Some kind of heavy equipment. He knew this was important, but wasn't sure why.

Blackstone was bleeding from several fairly serious wounds, but the Demon Lord was hurting more. Both stood panting on the screen. They had been fighting continuously for almost ninety minutes and both were exhausted. Gregory had to admire the attention to detail the game designers put into this. The Demon Lord suddenly leaped for Blackstone, trying to take him off guard, but he was ready, dodging the claws and burying his sword deep in the thing's shoulder. The Demon Lord bellowed in pain as the sun went out behind the blinds. Gregory flicked his eyes in that direction, loathe to take his eyes from the screen, but needing to know what was happening.

The sun was hiding behind an immense black wrecking ball on a thick chain. It smashed through his window and then blinds, taking out wood and drywall on either side. Time slowed down for Gregory. He watched individual shards of glass burst through the room, one of them stabbing him in the upper left arm, one missing his face by a quarter inch. The blinds, improbably remained attached to the wall, flipping up and rattling like tiny bones. Gregory could peripherally see the computer screen; Blackstone paused with his sword in the Demon Lord's shoulder. The Demon Lord, in Blackstone's moment of hesitation, clamped his mighty jaws over Blackstone's head, severing it from his body. Blood fountained upward on the screen. The wrecking ball came on through his apartment, digging a furrow in the floor. It came for Gregory as if he had somehow done it wrong. His hands were still on the computer, still trying to finish the game when the ball hit him. On the screen, the Demon Lord bellowed in triumph as Blackstone's body fell at its feet. At that moment, Gregory's body was crushed into pulp; his mind had time for one last thought:

I probably should've gotten off the couch.

✝

Ken MacGregor's *short stories have appeared (or will soon appear) in the anthologies:* A Quick Bite of Flesh, The Dead Sea, Heavy Metal Horror, Shithouse Tales *and* Erie Tales *(spelled like the lake intentionally); his work has also appeared in various magazines. Six of his screenplays were made into short films. He is a member in good standing of The Great Lakes Association of Horror Writers. He lives in Ypsilanti, Michigan with his brilliant wife Liz and astounding children Gabriel and Maggie. He drives the Bookmobile for the local Library. He can be found on Facebook*
(https://www.facebook.com/KenMacGregorAuthor?ref=hl), Amazon and Goodreads.

Mauschwitz

BRANDON FRENCH

The day you discover you are capable of hatred can be quite exhilarating. It means you no longer have to pretend to emulate Mother Teresa or Melanie Wilkes. You can be racist when the Korean woman in front of you is driving eleven miles an hour in the fast lane. You can be rude when two Seventh Day Adventists in unfashionable blue suits want to introduce you to Jesus. You can refuse to return phone calls to people who bore you, even if they're suicidal. And, you can walk past paraplegics, amputees and alcoholics without fumbling in your purse for a quarter.

The day I accepted how much I hated Ed Frankel, the monastery doors burst open. And when I learned a year later that he had died and I was glad, I burned my shirt. I was no longer going to feel ashamed of the devil who partied inside of me. After all, even Martin Luther admitted that Satan lived in his ass.

Ed Frankel, a short, muscular fellow with good hair and a tense jaw, got on my bad side when I was creative director of an ad agency that handled Disney's home video library, and he was "the client." I had encountered my share of asshole clients, as everyone does who works in advertising. There was the ice cream client who said our ads were too creative for a small space. There was the owner of a chain of health clubs who thought the black and white monitor he was watching meant that we weren't shooting his commercials in color. Then there was the deli owner who mistook the rough drawings of his mile-high sandwiches in the layouts for finished ads, yelling that we had made the meat look like shit. Not to mention the golf club client who fell asleep watching his expensive new 30-second commercial, "The Ball that Flew to the Moon." But Ed Frankel wasn't unsophisticated, cowardly or sleepy. He was a sadist.

"Let's see your latest waste of time and money," he'd say at the beginning of a meeting just as a warm-up insult. Our account executive Buddy Darrow would chuckle, mopping his bulbous red alcoholic's nose with a hanky as he accidentally spilled the storyboards onto the floor.

"What a kidder, Ed," I'd say, retrieving the storyboards and wishing that the scenery truck rumbling past the building was a prelude to The Big One.

On the day before Thanksgiving, Ed crowed, "Congratulations, Dani. You've managed to do the impossible. You've wrecked *Bambi!*"

The nicest thing Ed ever said about us was, "Well, you hire shit, you get shit. Go ahead and finish it."

It got so bad that once, after he kept us waiting in the hall for over two hours, I walked out, leaving poor, gin-starved Buddy and the creative team standing there with their mouths hanging open.

Of course, the general manager of our agency, Todd Berger, called me on the carpet the next day. He was rocking back and forth on his wingtips, his usually-tanned face as red as Buddy's nose.

"You had no right to walk out, Dani. I don't give a crap how long that putz kept you waiting."

"He's a miserable little freak, Todd. He hates the world and he takes it out on us."

"I don't care if he's the fuckin' queen of Romania, you have to stand there and take it. He's our second biggest client. He pays your salary!"

"Yes, I know. So we're just a bunch of whores, right?"

"Is that news?"

✝

Before Ed Frankel, I thought of Disney as a great opportunity. I had desperately wanted to be a Mousketeer like Annette Funicello when I was eight. And like most other kids in the 50's, I had grown up loving *Snow White, Pinnochio, Dumbo, Cinderella* and *Bambi*. What a privilege, I thought, to edit the footage of these masterpieces into irresistible four-color, thirty-second enticements. Bring Bambi Home! Let Dumbo Take You Flying! I was such a fan that it startled me when a disgruntled screenwriter dubbed Disney Studios "Mauschwitz." But Ed Frankel was my exit visa from Fantasyland.

I was not a happy camper when Todd Berger informed me that we — the agency *we* — were going to attend Ed Frankel's funeral, and that I — agency creative director — was going to write — and deliver — a tribute to the rotten sonovabitch.

"We are not going to lose this account just because Frankel is dead and some new asshole wants an agency that *he* has chosen! We are going to wow them with a great tribute that features our devotion to Disney Home Video, our beloved client. And you are going to make a winning wowee."

"A winning wowee?" I repeated, holding the phrase in my mouth like a spoiled oyster. "Gee, Todd, you're making me want to puke."

"Get over it."

✝

I sat in front of my computer, staring at the working title of the tribute: "Ding Dong. The Bitch is Dead." Where was Hannah Arendt when I needed her? Reaching into the trash for my compassion, I tried to think of Ed's grieving parents, but all I could conjure up were two drag queens, one sobbing sloppily, the other poking her in the ribs and shrieking, "Stop, Henrietta, stop!"

The Evil Queen from *Snow White* hallucinated her way into my office, wanting to be paid off for delivering Ed the poison apple. She leaned so close, I could smell her stringy hair and that awful sour perfume called "Old Flesh." I asked if she'd take a check.

Jake, the art director on the account, wandered into my office wearing a merciless little grin, his hair sticking straight up in the air like an Iroquois brave. "How's it going?"

"How do you think?"

"Yeah," Jake acknowledged, still grinning. He had purple jelly on the side of his mouth from the doughnut he was munching. "Did you know Ed died of AIDS?"

"Awww, shit, don't tell me that."

"Maybe it'll help you write the tribute," Jake said, pulling another doughnut out of a white deli bag.

"Thanks a bunch. Why couldn't he have been hit by a tour bus while crossing the lot to his car?"

"Nope, it was AIDS. Another one bites the dust, as Freddie Mercury would say."

"Go away, Jake.

Another one bites the dust. I liked that. Scrolling backwards to the working title, I changed it.

The ghost of Ollie floated in from the bright windows behind my desk, irresistibly seductive Ollie, dead at forty of AIDS. "Hi, kids," he said, dropping his lanky, prepped-out body into a convenient chair. "I'm bored. Make me laugh."

"Have you come to torment me?"

"How's your love life?"

"He dumped me."

"Awwwwww."

"I see that death has not improved your narcissism."

"What did you think of my memorial service?" he asked, wetting his finger with his tongue and rubbing a white spot off his Gucci loafer.

"It was a fifty share."

Crazy Cheryl, Ollie's favorite heterosexual playmate when he was screwing up his relationship with Peter, presided over the service, sporting a wacky purple hat with ostrich feathers and faux lynx fur that Ollie had picked out for her.

"Controlling everything as usual," she said, grabbing hold of the hat for emphasis. We all laughed, recalling with mixed emotions what a control freak he was. That was, in fact, what drove us apart. Ollie had insisted upon calling my married boyfriend Jeff to tell him to leave his wife for me and no amount of begging would stop him. I just couldn't handle his lunacy any longer, especially when I was being encouraged by a brace of therapists to grab hold of my sanity. I didn't know that he had been diagnosed with AIDS and was probably acting manic to avoid his terror of dying. I didn't realize when he knocked his water glass out of my hand at our favorite restaurant on Larchmont that he was trying to protect me from contagion. So I dropped him, and two years later he died without me. Fortunately, he had several hundred other friends, most of whom had stuck around, and they all piled into the big white church on Franklin Avenue for his memorial. When I looked around, the only significant person I didn't see was Peter.

I couldn't cry, even when I stood up to tell what had happened to us and how much I envied everyone else in the room for having thicker skins. But when Claire, Ollie's beloved—you should excuse the ex- pression—fag hag, lumbered over to hug me after the ceremony, with her hideously permed blond frizz and her two hundred and fifty pound body tightly packed into a yellow floral pup tent, I burst into tears, as if the pain of losing my closest friend had been warehoused somewhere out in Arcadia and required some time in a truck to be re- trieved. Or maybe I just needed somebody kind to hug me.

I looked back at the computer screen. It still said "Another one bites the dust." I pushed delete. Then I typed in "Sympathy for the Devil." Now I was really depressed, and it was all Ed Frankel's fault. Fuck him, I thought, and then felt guilty. Fuck that little weasel for dying of AIDS and making me feel bad for hating him.

✝

I wasn't sure how to dress for the Frankel memorial service. I decided on a navy blue suit with a white blouse, low heels, and pearls. In the bedroom mirror, I looked like the second most likely to succeed Republican candidate's wife. Actually, I looked like my ex-boyfriend Jeff's wife, except for the face. She was a proud Daughter of the American Revolution, a Martha Washington look-alike for whom pearls were a permanent scarification.

I couldn't eat, I was too nervous, but I thought I should shove something down my throat so that I didn't have a hypoglycemic attack and pass out while I was speaking. I settled for an apple, which turned out to be grainy and tasted like semi-sweet sand. I washed it down with a Diet Coke and emitted a loud belch.

"That was ladylike," I commented to the dog, feeling like an imposter in my church clothes.

✝

Parking was impossible, as it always is in West Hollywood. I couldn't even find a pay parking lot, just on-street metered parking, of which there was none available, and side street parking, which was illegal without a permit. I ended up leaving the car in a Pavilions lot six blocks from the church, going into the store and coming out another door in case a parking guard was watching.

I was late by the time I reached the church. The minister was already speaking about Ed and his beloved parents, Elsie and Donald Frankel. I strained to catch sight of them; neither was in drag.

I crept down a side aisle, looking for the familiar agency faces. They were twelve rows back, right off the aisle, and hadn't saved me a seat, the bastards. I found a single vacant one in the eleventh row and struggled to maneuver past the mourners without stepping on someone's foot.

Sighing with relief as I settled into the seat, I turned to look at Todd. He shook his head and squeezed his mouth into a disapproving smirk. Jake was grinning at me like a caged monkey, his diarrhea-brown sport jacket straining to hold his belly in place.

There didn't seem to be any formal order for the speakers. Each one walked down front, stepped onto a raised dais, spoke, and returned to his seat, followed by a pause until the next person got up. If I waited long enough, I thought desperately, perhaps the minister would end the service before I could speak.

But Todd had no intention of letting that happen. He tapped me sharply on the shoulder and whispered, "Get your ass down there." I started to rise, but then someone else appeared at the front of the church. He looked to be in his early thirties with a thin face made thinner by a blond brush cut. Was this Ed's lover? He was wearing a black suit, white shirt and a red plaid bow-tie, which made him look like grandma's favorite little boy, or an undertaker. It was hard to hear him because he spoke softly, but I caught some of it. *Ed was an amazing friend who was always there to listen whenever he needed him.* *Ed?* Was he kidding? Then he said that Ed had been very brave about the diagnosis, maintaining his sense of humor even when his t-cell count dipped below a hundred. Ed had a sense of humor? He said that he loved Ed and would probably never find a better friend. He started to cry a little. Feeling embarrassed, I looked down at my lap, discovering that I had unwittingly shredded part of the little speech I had prepared. But I could still make out most of the words; it was just the paper that looked damp and worm-eaten.

When Ed's friend finished speaking, Todd poked me in the neck with his finger. I shot up, stumbled over to the aisle, and started to walk forward. My legs were shaking. Oh my God, this was going to be a disaster.

At the dais, I tried to smooth out the paper. My hands were shaking as badly as my legs. People started to cough uncomfortably. Adjusting the microphone, I forced myself to speak.

"My name is Dani Lauer. I am the creative director at Sweeney and Markowitz, the agency which handles the Disney Home Video account. Ed Frankel was my client." My voice sounded shrill and wobbly, like Eleanor Roosevelt's. I took a deep breath.

"We were thrilled to have the privilege of working on such masterpieces as *Snow White*, *Pinnochio* and *Cinderella*. Ed was a very demanding boss, asking for our very finest work and never settling for less. The payoff was that Disney Home Video scored a hit every time an animation classic was released." Todd had made me put that in, to remind the Disney execs what a great job we'd done for them.

The next line was, "We will miss Ed." I started to say it, but I couldn't finish. Everything became blurry and I felt light-headed. Then something gushed out of me like an episode of *I Didn't Know I was Pregnant*.

"Listening to Ed's friends speak about him today, I realize that I... didn't really know him. To be honest," I said, wondering what I was going to be honest about, "the Ed I knew was—well, he could be very…harsh." My legs had stopped shaking, but I couldn't bring my-self to look up from the paper I was no longer reading. "I think that Ed —well, he never minced words with me. So—today I haven't, either. Maybe he would have liked that." There was really nothing left to say. "Thank you very much for letting me speak. I am really, uh…very sorry for your loss."

The oxygen began returning to my brain. Oh my god, I thought, I'm going to be fired. Avoiding everyone's gaze, I hurried back to my seat, stumbling on the carpet and nearly falling before a man grabbed my arm to steady me. I glanced at him for a second, grateful. He nodded and gave me a little smile.

When I sat down again, I began to cry. I couldn't stop the tears, but I struggled not to make a sound. I felt a hand gently squeeze my shoulder. I patted the hand without turning around.

✝

I didn't lose my job. And we didn't lose the account. A woman named Harriet took over for Ed and everything went on as if nothing had happened. Advertising was like that. People came and went, dropping off the edge of the world like it was really flat after all, and it didn't seem to matter if they were important or not, everyone went over the edge eventually, blip-blip-blip.

I didn't particularly like Harriet, she wasn't smart like Ed and didn't push us very hard. But she was never mean, just dim. Her highest praise was, "That's cute." Jake began using that expression whenever we presented something internally. "Oh, that's so cute," he would shriek, "isn't that the cutest thing?"

✝

I don't usually think about Ed unless I bump into one of the old Dis-ney classics. Then I remember something cutting he said to me, like "Well, Snow White you're not," but it doesn't bother me like it used to. Mauschwitz is gone, at least for me, deserted and windblown like any disaster area reinvented by time; all the bodies are buried in the ash pond and a ragged grass has taken over. I have made my peace with Disney as the not-so-magical kingdom. I have even resumed a half-hearted quest to emulate Melanie Wilkes, or Mother Teresa—but only after she admitted that she had lost her faith. To be honest, I miss how exhilarating it felt to be a real sonovabitch for a while. Ed gave me that. He was like a colon cleanse that swept out all the bullshit-caked pipes, the politically correct orifices, and scrubbed them honest. Maybe that's what bad guys do for us. Maybe that's why we hold onto them—Satan for the Christians, Hitler for the Jews, the Mafia for all of us who crave a little anarchy. It's like Oppenheimer said after the first atom bomb test, "Now we're all sons of bitches."

Let's face it, the dark side is a far more popular vacation resort than Disney World. It might not be a bad idea to purchase a timeshare there.

✝

Brandon French *is the only daughter of an opera singer and a Spanish dancer, born during a shortage of bananas at the end of the Second World War. She began writing stories at the age of three, mostly about getting a pony or a puppy.*